SLOW BURN

By
J.J. Massa

Published by
Melange Books, LLC
White Bear Lake, MN 55110
www.melange-books.com

Slow Burn Digest, J.J. Massa, Copyright © 2007-2009, 2011
ISBN 978-1-61235-134-6

Credits

Editor: Nancy Schumacher
Copy Editor: Taylor Evans
Format Editor: Mae Powers
Cover Artist: A. Bratt

SLOW BURN
J.J. Massa

Old Friends
Evie and Gibb have known each other for more than a decade. It's about time for these two longtime friends to negotiate a new relationship—hopefully, it won't be at the cost of the rest of their old friends.

Teacher, Teacher
Krayton Vance and Vivian Talon had several things in common. They both worked for the public education system, they both decided to spend their Spring Break in Spain, and they're both looking for a fling. The question is, what happens to them when the break is over?

Dinner for One
What could be lonelier than dinner by oneself? Many things, as it turns out. Join Maura for a memorable evening of dinner, drinks, and meeting new people. It's a meal she will always remember.

Anything
Intoxicated by a beautiful voice and a meaningful song, centuries old vampire Amedeo Di Calibria searches to find the singer. He finds beautiful but emotionally frozen Alexa. Can he melt the ice around her heart?

Counting Midnight, Vampire Novel
Mélange Digest (Short Story: Nailed)
Montgomery Werewolves 1: Acting Like Family

Old Friends
By JJ Massa

Chapter One

"Okay, that's a wrap then, people!"

"Thank God!" Evie mumbled, clutching the broad, solid shoulders of the man she'd just spent six hours with, doing the same three scenes over and over.

"You said it, love," sighed her co-star, slipping from the cultured accent he affected for the show into a slightly more course sounding London slang. "I'm for a cuppa tea, followed closely by a double shot of some fine malt. I'd 'ave a pint, but who can drink that horse piss you yanks call beer?"

"Give it a rest, ya *berk*," she snarked, elbowing the tall, muscular man in the ribs.

"'ay! I wish I never taught you such! You're a cheeky thing, you are!"

The two argued good-naturedly until they parted company on the edge of the set area, the man heading toward the right and Evie to the left.

Marla, her assistant, was waiting for her when Evie walked into her dressing room. "Your *husband* called twice," she sneered at the title, twisting the cap off a bottle of sparkling water brutally. "And someone named Josie said to call her back," she added in a friendlier tone.

"Thanks, Marla." Evie sank into a cushioned chair and tucked her feet beneath her. "I'm going to call Josie. I just don't have what it takes to talk to Ritchie right now."

"Mm, hmm," Marla mumbled noncommittally, dabbing at the heavy makeup on Evie's face while Evie dialed Josie's number. This was a daily routine for the two now.

"Hey!" Josie answered, her voice loud and strong.

"Hey." Evie grinned. Wonderful Josie. Some things never changed.

"Hey!" Josie countered back, voice flat. This was how it always went when she called Josie.

"Hey," Evie responded. She knew her smile sounded in her voice

4

"Hey!" Josie said again, unflappable.

"All right, you win," Evie chuckled. They would be saying nothing more than *hey* for ten minutes if she didn't give. But it was fun. Josie was fun. Fun and strong, and always there for her—no matter what.

"Okay, okay, so...did he bite your throat?" Josie gushed, sounding a lot like a fan-girl and nothing like the almost-forty year old executive's wife and pillar of the community that she was.

"Who? Trent?" Evie shook her head at the phone, shifting so that Marla could swab at the red gel simulating blood on her neck. "Of course he bit me—about a million times! The entire show is based on the premise of him biting my throat—sucking my blood. It's kind of icky after awhile. I'm sure your husband biting you is more romantic than..."

"Don't talk crazy, woman!" Josie yelped. "Trent Worthington is hot. There is no comparison between my husband and a hunky, famous TV star sucking on my throat."

"You've been married to him for twenty years and you don't like Luke biting your throat?" Evie angled her head out of the way so that Marla could rub a little arnica into the bruise at her jugular. She'd have a permanent hickie by the end of next season, she was sure of it. "Is that why you called? To ask me about Trent, AKA Dragos, the emotionally torn vampire?"

"Was that a shot?" Josie asked suspiciously. "Because if that was a shot, you can't come to my new, obscenely huge, and luxurious beach house." She paused. When Evie didn't answer, she went on. "Everyone's coming. Between me, Tricia, and Clay, I think we've got the whole gang showing up over the course of the next two weeks. Just in time for your show's hiatus."

"Really? Everyone?" Evie waved Marla off with an apologetic smile, sitting up straight. "Uh, Sam, Randy, Gibb...Gibb and Dora? And the rest?"

"Yep, the whole gang. Don't know if Gibb and Dori will be there, but most of 'em have all called or e-mailed. Gibb's my next call. One or two might not make it...but just about everyone will be there over the course of the next week or so."

Gibb. Why did she always stop at Gibb? Evie gave herself a little shake. The last thing she needed was to indulge her old crush right now. Either way, she'd have fun. And she liked Dora, Gibb's wife, well enough. She could watch Gibb covertly and have a fun relaxing time at the beach. If he didn't make it, she'd still have a great time in the company of all of her old friends.

"Filming for this season just wrapped. I was going to escape on my own for a little while," Evie mused aloud to Josie. "I don't have to worry about Ritchie and the kids—they're off to Disney World for the week."

"Good, come whenever you want," Josie said airily, taking Evie's vague speculation as assent. "If you can get away tomorrow, I plan to get down there early. We can have a couple of days to ourselves. It's going to take that long to talk about everybody. There's Lani and Karl's breakup—can you believe he came out of the closet like that?" Josie gasped, mentioning two friends who had been part of their crowd for years.

"I'm still reeling over that one...not that there's anything wrong with that!" Evie giggled, quoting a line from a popular TV show. "And I guess Randy's still growling about Deb starting that home business. It's pretty cool about the picture Erik took being used on that Greatest Hits of the Millennium CD, though."

"I think Leah had something to do with that." Leah was a concert promoter and Evie knew that CDs and concerts happened in two very different venues. She'd bring that up with Josie another time. For now, Josie was still speaking and Evie was enjoying the conversation more than any she'd had in awhile. "So far I've got yeses from Sam and Sarah, Tricia and Lynne, Clay, Randy and Deb, you, and I'm about to call Gibb." Josie paused. "Um, he's not around there anywhere, is he?"

Evie laughed. "Josie, I don't even know if he works on TV shows anymore...I do know he writes movies—big, big movies. For all I know, he's on location somewhere. I'm in Connecticut right now."

"Fine, fine," Josie growled. "I still believe it's all going on in one huge building in Paramus, but you keep your little show biz secrets. I'll call him myself. I'll call ya later! Bye!"

And that was Josie for you. Evie shook her head and laughed to herself as she snapped her cell phone closed.

"Well, Marla." She grinned at her assistant. "Looks like I'm going to the beach."

* * * *

"Gibb Weston!" Gibb barked into his cell as he slid behind the wheel of his car. He'd briefly considered ignoring it, but it could be important.

"Well, *you* sound cranky!"

Gibb grinned, for the first time in longer than he could remember. "Josie! How the hell are you?"

"Better than you, apparently. I'm not biting my friend's heads off whenever my phone rings. You need some beach time!"

"I wish I could," he sighed. "Now isn't a great time."

"Oh, come on!" she wheedled. "There's no bad time to come to the beach. And besides, Luke just bought us this huge, decadent beach house—he says it's an investment. So I'm investing his hard earned money into a crazy, honkin', week-long beach party. Everyone's coming. You gotta come!"

Gibb turned the key, starting his car, though he didn't put it in gear. "Everyone? When?" He was weakening. Why couldn't he go to the beach with all his old friends? Didn't he deserve a little comfort and fun?

"Yup, everyone. You know you wanna hear about the latest video game Tricia's peddling. And I know Sam's got some good pool installation stories for you. We're a very inspiring crowd. You could write a movie about us."

"I'm sure I could," Gibb chuckled. "Enough beer and I'm always inspired." He was definitely warming up to the idea. "So when is everyone showing up? Is the whole gang coming?"

"Just about," Josie assured him. "I've already confirmed Sam and Sarah, Tricia and Lynne, Clay, Randy and Deb, you if you'll just quit arguing…" she trailed off and Gibb could hear her tapping away for a moment or two. "Okay, I just got an email from Leah and one from Karl. They'll both be there on Monday."

"It would be good to see everyone," he murmured. "I just have so much going on right now."

"Okay, Mr. Important Screen Writer. But if Evie can drag herself away from that hunky vampire she's got sucking on her neck every week and visit us little people, you'd think you could force yourself," Josie sniped.

"Oh, you talked to Evie, huh? The show wrapped already?" he asked casually. He hoped he sounded offhand. Try as he might, he'd never been indifferent to Evie.

"How long does it take to get caught by a vampire over and over again? Although I've gotta give her credit. She makes it look different every single time. I think it's the clothes," Josie speculated, apparently giving it due consideration. "Anyway, she's managed to unload Bitchy Ritchie and his ankle snappers. We're gonna get there tomorrow and drink a lot while we bad-mouth the rest of you guys. Everyone else will be showing up Sunday or Monday."

"Hmm." He pretended to think it over. "Plenty of beer? Beach music?"

"Chuh, yeah! Duh. Who do you think you're talking to, buddy?" Josie squawked. "Good food, good booze, good music, and good friends. And I don't wanna hear any *chit* from you! You coming or ain't ya?"

Of course he would. He'd been tempted in the first place, but Evie had sealed the deal. Not that he would tell Josie—or anyone else that.

"All right, I'll be there. Dora can't make it, though." Dora had had a bulimic relapse. That was something else he didn't plan on mentioning.

"We'll just have to make due with you, I guess. Okay, I got other calls to make. Talk at ya later."

That was the end of that conversation. Gibb looked in bemusement at his cell. Well, all right, then. He was going to the beach.

* * * *

"I'm a damned fool," Gibb Weston muttered to himself. "A damned stupid fool."

He'd paused at the door leading onto a wide wooden porch overlooking the ocean, shaking his head at his own self-delusion. During the two-hour flight from New York he'd identified and catalogued his guilt—or so he'd thought. He'd convinced himself that it was the direct result of leaving his estranged wife at a behavioral health clinic while he went off to play with his old friends.

One look at the petite and shapely woman lounging on the colorful chaise staring off into the middle distance and he couldn't hide from this particular truth any longer. Long dark hair framed an oval face, pensive shadows tinting below large brown eyes. They'd known each other for so long—danced around each other the entire time. Had he known she would be here alone? Yes, he had. Josie had sent out a group email about her own later-than-planned arrival. Facts were facts. He'd come early knowing it would be just the two of them for at least a day—a day and a night.

8

"Gibb?" Evie's husky light voice was hesitant, bringing him forward, through the French doors and out. "Gibb!" she yelped, rising gracefully to her feet, unguarded delight in her smile.

His long legs made short work of the space between them and then she was in his arms. "Evie, my god it's good to see you," he murmured, leaning down. He meant to kiss her cheek, a chaste peck, nothing more.

Before he could manage even that much, she wrapped both arms around him, buried her face in his chest and burst into tears. Somewhere between rage at whatever had caused this upset and a driving need to make what was wrong right again, Gibb knew he was in serious trouble.

"I'm sorry, I'm sorry," she whispered seconds later, her voice twice as raspy and three times as sexy for it. "I'm just so tired, that's all." She tilted her head back and looked up at him, all pale cheeks, luminous brown eyes and soft, full lips. "There's just so much going on. It's good to see you, Gibb."

Gibb groaned inwardly, sinking down to a wide lounger, pulling her with him. He scooted backward, finding the angled cushion behind to lean against and situated her on his lap.

"You okay now?" he asked, bending one leg so that she could use it as extra support.

"I really am. Honest," she sighed, her head nestling into the hollow just below his clavicle. A perfect fit. "The dailies went long on the final episode for the show and then Ritchie and the kids lost their tickets... By the time I got out this morning, I was ready to mortgage the house and rent them an entire theme park for the week."

"Oh, yeah." Gibb smiled wryly. "Your husband and his kids. I almost forgot." Pressing a kiss into her hair he asked, "So, how are they? Is he working yet?"

She shifted against him, looking into his eyes, her own smile crooked and ironic. "Ritchie working? Not happening. How's Dora? Any better?"

"Inpatient right now." He shrugged. "Sometimes she's better, sometimes she's not."

Turning to face forward, Evie settled against him. "We're quite a pair, aren't we? Barely exchanging two words when we're with the old crowd, working in the same industry but we don't speak. And look at us now."

Tightening his arms around her, Gibb inhaled a deep breath of her light scent and released it, not knowing what he should say. There was plenty he could tell her, but wouldn't. "Maybe discretion really is the better part of valor," he murmured, petting a hand over her long, satiny hair.

"Maybe," she agreed. Angling her head slightly, she arched a delicate brow at him. "So how valiant are you feeling right this minute?"

Another little shift brought his erection against her lower back, answering the question for both of them. "Shit," he growled, tilting his head against the lounger's cushion.

"Supper out?" she asked sheepishly, scooting away from him on the chaise.

"Good idea." He nodded, unfolding himself stiffly. "I'll just grab my luggage and meet you back down in a few minutes. When should we expect everyone else?"

"I'll go up with you," she countered, waiting for him as he headed for the front door, retrieving his two suitcases and a garment bag. Walking up the stairs, she filled him in on their friends' agenda. "I think you and I are it for the next two days. Josie wanted to come in the morning but instead it'll be day after tomorrow, since Luke can't get away. Tricia thought she and Lynn would make it tomorrow, but now they can't. What's wrong?" she asked when he stopped in the hallway and looked at her.

"Did you notice the room assignments?" Gibb asked, tapping a square of paper affixed to her door.

Evie grinned, looking at the little square with her name written on it. "Yeah. Cute, isn't it? There's some reason for every room, too, according to Josie," she laughed. "Mine is because the bed in this room is extra soft and I'm apparently a lightweight and a whiner." She swept an arm toward the room across the hall. "Tricia's room is over there—something to do with claustrophobia and big windows," she explained vaguely. "Josie's a nut, huh?"

"Hmm," Gibb answered noncommittally, heading on down the hall to the next room. He could have used the connecting door, though Evie seemed not to have noticed it yet. He had a feeling it would come to haunt him relentlessly during the rest of their stay.

Chapter Two

Evie closed her eyes, enjoying the light shore breeze playing through her hair. Good food and good company, she couldn't ask for more than that. Sitting there in the gathering dusk, she was looking forward to both.

Gibb had excused himself after they ordered and walked a little way down the pier to make a phone call. Though she couldn't hear exactly what he was saying, Evie enjoyed the light stroke of his smooth southern accent as it carried across the short distance. If she were honest, she more than enjoyed it. Maybe she wasn't ready for that much honesty right now.

She watched him as he turned, pacing several feet and pivoting gracefully around, all but stalking back toward her. *Mmmm...* The setting sun sparked brassy highlights in his long auburn hair, bringing it to life. Worn in a neatly secured tail, he reached up and tucked an escaped strand behind his ear, tipping his head in response to what he was hearing on the phone.

Gibb Weston was an attractive man, Evie didn't mind admitting that. Her own husband, Ritchie, was classically handsome and muscular, almost magazine ad pretty. Gibb was tall, thin, but well built, his face angular, with razor sharp cheekbones and a full mouth. Evie gave herself a firm mental shake, smiling at the waitress as she poured a glass of wine, leaving a small carafe behind. Gibb was her friend. She needed to get her eyes and her mind off his mouth.

"Oh, yeah," Gibb groaned, surprising her with his sudden appearance and slipping into his seat opposite her to take a healthy swallow of his beer. "That's the best beer I've had in my entire life," he swore, emptying half of it.

"Gearing up for Josie?" Evie giggled, lifting her glass for another sip of wine.

"I'm so damned glad to be here, Ev," Gibb sighed. "You have no idea."

"I do know, Gibb..." She smiled. "I really do."

Gibb considered her for a long minute before reaching across the table, covering her hand. "We've never been close, Evie, but I've always felt connected to you. Talk to me, friend."

Evie looked down at their joined hands, the long fingers twined with hers, and then into his intense sky blue gaze. "I've...me too,

11

Gibb. I always hang out with Josie, and Tricia and I were friends before anyone. But you and me...I don't know. It's a little odd, isn't it?"

"Talk to me, love," he insisted, giving her hand a squeeze. "What aren't you saying?"

"Ritchie and I...well, I've got some kind of neuro-thing so I'm tired a lot more. It affects my hand strength, things like that. That's why I'm taking this vacation—not taking another role right now," she blurted, bracing herself for his reaction.

Gibb shook his head one time. "Ritchie and you...Neuro-thing? Ev, what kind of neuro-thing?"

"You're squeezing too tight," Evie murmured.

Gibb lifted her fingers to his mouth, gently kissing the knuckle. "I'm sorry, Ev, but you can't leave me hanging. I care, you know that."

She nodded, fighting tears. People assumed, since she was quasi-famous, that she was cared for, looked after somehow. It wasn't that she wasn't loved, but Gibb made her feel cosseted, at least a little. The rest of the time, she was the care-giver, the doer.

"It's not that big a deal," she began. Gibb arched a dark copper brow and refused to budge. "Something about the flu shot I got in November reacted badly with my peripheral nerves. I get fatigued easily. But I'm taking vitamin therapy for it. It's supposed to improve over time. It's really not *that* big a thing. I do what the doctor says and I'm fine."

He swept his thumb down the backs of her fingers. "And Ritchie? How's he dealing with this?"

Evie took a deep breath. Here was the crux of the matter. "You can't tell Josie about this...especially about Ritchie. She hates Ritchie...I'll tell her about it when it seems like a good time."

Both eyebrows were creeping toward his hairline now and his forehead was furrowed with concern. "Evie, *what* is going on?" he asked insistently.

"Ritchie and I are—have been, separated, the divorce is nearly final," she admitted. "He felt it was too much for the kids and...well he couldn't give them the care they needed if he had to take care of me...and stuff," she sighed glancing away.

Evie really didn't want to look at his face as she tried to excuse her ex-husband. It wasn't as if she didn't know what Ritchie was like.

"But you're still supporting him, because he's got those kids and all, huh?" Gibb mused, sweeping his thumb across the back of her hand again. She shrugged and then nodded, looking down at her plate when the waitress slid it in front of her, not sure she could eat a thing. He tipped her face up, two fingers under her chin. Summer blue eyes locked on hers, he told her, "Dora asked me for a divorce—she'd already filed. After that, she went on a binge and purge spree. Now she's in a forced care facility. Let's not tell Josie that either."

Evie couldn't look away. Gibb leaned slowly forward until his lips touched hers. Soft, sensual, slow, he lingered there for long seconds, just feeling, resting against her. Satin warm, his tongue flicked against her lower lip and away. A promise.

"Drink your wine, Evie. I'm getting another beer," he murmured when he pulled back. His voice sounded a little strained to her and she smiled slightly, lifting her glass as ordered.

"Aren't you Eve St. John? Ohmigod! It's Eve St. John!" a woman called out, looming over her. "I just *love* your show. Look, Bob! It's Eve St. John! From *Life's Blood*, my favorite show!"

"As soon as we eat, she'll sign whatever," Gibb promised, edging his chair around the table. "Just leave it here, okay?" He smiled up at the woman, placing himself between Evie and the enthusiastic fan. "You have any cards or anything, Ev?" he asked in a low voice.

Evie nodded, grateful for his quick thinking. She'd forgotten the advice that had led her to sign a handful of picture cards and toss them into her bag. Gibb had been achieving his own level of success and knew the ropes. She'd spent a fair amount of time paying attention to him, watching him become more and more sought after as a screen writer, and had felt a quiet pride while climbing her own ladder of success.

She handed Gibb the few cards in her purse and he passed one to the woman who reached over and shook Evie's hand, gushing as she walked off.

"I'm so sorry," the waitress apologized. "I didn't recognize you when you came in, and ..."

"It's fine, honestly," Evie assured her. "I'm just here to eat." She smiled, taking a token bite of her food. She was pretty sure she wouldn't really be able to eat, but she didn't want the girl to feel bad.

"Do you mind wrapping this up?" Gibb asked, a nod toward the two almost untouched plates of food. "I think we'll make it an early night, don't you, love?"

Evie didn't know what might be crossing Gibb's mind right then, but his low tone caressed her nerves like soft silk, teasing her, making her tingle all over.

"Yes," she croaked, clearing her throat. "Yeah, an early night," she agreed, nodding like an idiot.

* * * *

"Ritchie, what if you talked to her boyfriend? I'm sure she wants to see the kids." Evie's voice sounded reasonable, if strained. She'd been on the phone with her dead-beat ex for ten minutes and the circles under her eyes were darker than ever.

"Evie?" Gibb called in a low voice, holding a glass of wine out to her. She reached for it and he caught her hand. "Say goodbye," he dictated, withholding the drink from her. For a moment, he was sure she would turn away and keep talking.

"Ritchie, I've got to go," she said firmly into the phone.

Before Ritchie could finish his objection, which Gibb could hear quite clearly from a few feet away, Gibb snatched the cell phone and closed it, opening it again to press the red button, turning the thing off.

"They're his kids, it's his ex-wife, and he's right there," Gibb explained. "You were talking in circles. He's wearing you out, Ev."

He didn't really feel guilty. If anything, he was annoyed. He didn't have any clear cut plan for them besides being alone together for maybe the first time ever. What he didn't want was her loser ex-ish husband making her exhausted before they could even have a decent conversation.

"You're right, Gibb," she sighed. "It's habit as much as anything."

Gibb grabbed a second glass and the open bottle of Shiraz. "Let's take this down to the beach, huh?" He grinned, sliding an arm around her waist and turning her toward the door.

She moved with him as if they'd been doing it for years, turning, walking in step, slowing just enough to kick her shoes off at the bottom of the stairs. Gibb knew a good idea when he saw one and kicked his shoes off, too.

Somehow, the two made it through the shifting sand and down without even stumbling. Gibb couldn't ignore how perfectly she fit against his side though she was almost ten inches shorter than he was. Her body snugged well next to his and she felt right.

"This spot works," Evie mumbled shyly, kicking up a little plume of sand.

"Perfect," Gibb agreed, plopping down and pulling her along beside him.

Snuggling against him, Evie held her wineglass aloft and let him top it off, waiting for him to fill his own as well.

They sat in silence for a moment, holding hands, sipping their wine as they watched the waves from halfway down a large sand dune. With dusk had come the gentle decline in temperature, from the high eighties to a balmy seventy-six. The air was lightly warm, welcoming, dark like a weightless blanket floating in and out with the rolling tide.

"Tell me something about you that everyone *should* already know, but doesn't," Gibb murmured, his deep voice blending with the music of the ocean.

Evie squirmed back against him, settling in. His hand on her stomach kept her close.

"Hmm, lessee," she mused, sipping her wine. "I don't like conflict-I hate to argue." She growled lightly, "And people always want *me* to be the one talking to angry people. It makes no sense. There! I've said it."

Looking up at him, her smile was one of liberation and he couldn't help but grin back. Such a simple thing, but she never felt like telling anyone. An elbow to his rib and an arched brow told him it was his turn.

"Thomas Jefferson is my favorite president," he said resolutely, with a solid nod.

"Uh, okay, but why should everyone know that about you?" she asked, confusion clear on her face.

"I write him into everything I do." His own brow arched now, he waited, watching the wheels turn behind her eyes.

Her breath caught. "You do! Every movie, every show, someone mentions Thomas Jefferson. How cool is *that*?" she crowed, climbing to her knees and facing him.

"It's very cool," he murmured, reaching up to cup her face. "Tell me something about your life that you keep quiet," he mumbled, leaning in to kiss her cheek.

Shifting back on the sand, he sipped his wine. She sat down on her shins, resting, and sipped her own wine, considering.

"Ritchie's kids are obnoxious, sometimes, and so's he. I'd pay a lot if *he* would just get a girlfriend." She sighed. "Your turn."

He nodded, knowing, even relieved to admit aloud what he'd kept so close that he wouldn't even tell himself. "Dora's condition scares me. I kind of love her, but I don't know if I can deal with her…only it would be wrong to let her do it by herself, even if we do divorce."

They regarded one another solemnly, at the line, about to cross. "Tell me what you want, right this minute, more than anything else," Evie whispered, her husky voice smoky, enticing.

"You, completely," Gibb rasped, unmoving, straining against an invisible barrier.

"Me, too," she managed, and the barrier was gone.

Chapter Three

Evie knew that Gibb had risen with her, some kind of choreographed dance. Reaching for him, she wasn't surprised when he pulled her in, fingers threaded as she pressed against him.

He opened his mouth as if to speak, thought better of it and leaned over her. Pushing up against his hands, she stood on tiptoes, face to face with him. His eyes were intense, bolts of blue lightning against the fabric of a summer sky, hot and riveting.

She moved against him as he lowered his head, no teasing now. Masculine lips covered hers, warm, demanding, insistent as his tongue swept her willing mouth.

A new space opened inside her, pulling her in as she savored his unique flavor: red, red wine, wild summer oceans and spicy Gibb—Evie was quickly addicted. She held onto him, tasting, feeling, she was drunk on his heady flavor now and so little had happened yet. Knowing that there was more to come was nearly overwhelming as they made their way up the beach, kissing, stumbling as they went.

Amazing. Blown away. Overwhelmed. And they'd just barely touched. What would happen when they made love? And they would…were going to, were minutes away. The idea of it made Evie's knees weak and she stumbled over the threshold.

"You still with me?" he rumbled, his arm around her back.

They were on the stairs now, she could make it that little bit further. "Fine," she agreed, moving on automatic, eager like she'd never been before.

And then she was under him, the soft down of the comforter against her back, his hard body above her, her fingers searching through his shirt, making short work of buttons. His mouth covered hers, devouring, sucking, her hands tracing his angular face, the sky blue fire of his eyes looking into her, finding, keeping what he wanted. More, just more, his long thin fingers flicking away buttons, parted fabric, searched, and found smooth, warm skin.

"Gibb," she breathed, not sure what she was even saying as she tugged at his jeans, kicking out of her brief skirt with his help, straining toward him like a flower seeking the sun.

"Oh, yeah," he groaned, scooting them both up the bed and leaving his jeans and shorts behind.

Skin on skin, sliding against each other. Evie stroked up Gibb's leanly muscled ribcage loving the sleek powerful feel of him. His thick erection prodded her hip as they rolled again on the bed so that she rested on top of him, his hands cupping her rear.

"You feel so good," he murmured, mouthing against her throat.

"You, too," she husked, one leg falling between his as she angled her neck so that he would have better access. "Oh, god, I can't believe how good you feel."

"Mmm, and it's about to get even better."

One hand covered her breast, kneading and rolling a nipple, only to slip down over her taut belly, combing through the tight curls over her mound. His fingers parted her labia, pressing lightly against her engorged clit, then a little harder, back and forth, leaving her gasping.

His lips covered hers, wet and warm, his tongue caressing her palate as they rolled one more time. With his free hand, Gibb pulled her knee up, over his hip, guiding the tip of his cock to her hot center.

"Gibb," she panted, trying to say something, not sure what.

He dragged the wide head between her slick folds-once, twice, and then pulled back.

"Condom," he rasped, almost choking on it.

"Oh." Yes, that's what she'd been trying to remember. A condom. Safe sex. Very important. For some reason…

He stretched across her, fumbling, and then producing one from somewhere. "I'll hold this," he rasped. "Tear the top off and you can put it on me."

Normally, Evie knew she would be a little nervous—she wasn't the most sexually sophisticated person out there. Right now, though, she felt confident, sexy, sure of herself. She leaned up to kiss him lightly, took the corner of the little packet between her thumb and forefinger and tugged. Once opened, she pulled the pink rubber disk out, her other hand reaching down to stroke the steely soft length between Gibb's legs.

"You sure it'll fit?" She wrinkled her nose at him, squeezing him lightly.

"Oh, god, I hope so," he groaned, spreading his legs a little wider. "If you don't quit doing that and put it on there, woman, it'll be surplus any minute now."

Evie barely recognized her breathless giggle, holding his cock in one hand and rolling the condom down over it with the other.

With a groan, Gibb stretched over her, his hands sweeping up from her hips, over her ribcage, under her arms and up. Pulling her arms and hands above her head, he pinned both wrists in one hand, spreading her legs with an impatient knee.

"You ready, Evie?" he whispered, nipping at her chin.

"Yes. Please," she gasped back, arching up into him.

She felt his hand slip between them, the back of it against her stomach and mound as he guided himself to her creaming sheath and slowly began to push in. Seated fully inside her, he leaned up to look into her eyes. The intense blue flame of his gaze held her frozen and breathless, unable to do more than stare back at him. Eyes locked, he pulled back until only the tip of his throbbing cock brushed her center. She arched, hips seeking greater contact and he gave it to her, plunging deep, wrapping his arms around her. Writhing against him, she clutched at his shoulders, her fingernails digging. In and out, deeper and deeper he thrust into her, filling her completely with every stroke. With her legs wrapped around his waist, his tight pubic curls teased and tugged at her clit. She clung to him, crying out with every plunge, not even trying to keep up as he took her higher and higher.

"So good, Evie," he panted. "Gonna come…"

Grinding against him, Evie bit down on his shoulder, hiding a scream as her vaginal muscles clamped tight, over and over again. White spots edged the corners of her vision and all she could do was hang there, holding on.

* * * *

Gibb didn't know what woke him up. It could have been the dim pearly light sneaking past the slatted shades. Maybe the sound of seabirds wheeling outside penetrated his sleepy fog.

Evie snuffled sweetly against him and he couldn't help but smile. She was stunning in full make up and beautiful the rest of the time. Right now with her hands curled under her chin and her hair fanning over one naked shoulder, she was both beautiful and cute. Cutely beautiful? It didn't matter.

Carefully, Gibb slid out of the bed, looking around. They'd come to her room last night, it being the first along the hall. That connecting door was going to be more than a little convenient, starting right now.

In a matter of minutes, he was dressed for a run, the used condom wrapped in tissue in his pocket so that he could throw it away in a trash can further down the beach. He didn't bother with the front door. A run along the sand would suit his needs perfectly.

Even if the others did arrive, they wouldn't catch him crawling out of Evie's bed. Right now, he wanted nothing more than to savor the dawn serenity and enjoy the calm satisfaction of the morning after some very good sex. He didn't know what this thing was between the two of them, but after scratching the itch that had burned for more than a decade, Gibb could at least admit they'd been fighting a powerful attraction. No doubt, Evie would admit it as well.

Would she see hearts and flowers? Was she still in love with Ritchie? How did he feel about Dora? And did any of that matter? A night or two of good sex between lifelong friends did not equal wedding invitations. Gibb shook his head and snickered at himself. If he kept on this way, he'd certainly lose any peace he'd found overnight. If ever an occasion screamed, *"seize the day",* this one did.

* * * *

"Well, well, well!" A strident voice jerked Evie unceremoniously awake.

She sat straight up, shocked and disoriented. Where was she? Who was carrying on? Gibb! Oh yeah, Gibb had been…there.

The bed was still warm, and if Josie moved around the other side to open the curtains, who knew what she'd find?

"Uh, Josie? Hi!" she managed weakly. "What time did you get here?"

"Late enough to miss you and Gibb all snug in the bed, but early enough to see that you just slept in the same one—if slept is the right word here," Josie announced pulling no punches.

"Um, well, I guess he went out…maybe he made his bed first…" she started, only to be cut off smartly.

"Don't even try it, girlfriend!" Josie warned her, hands on her hips. "The only reason I didn't catch you in the bed together is because one of you shut the door. His room and all the others were wide open. Don't *even* try to tell me that one of you slept on the floor or something." She paused and looked around. "Besides, the whole room smells like sex!" she announced.

"Josie, do you mind?" Evie was beginning to get a little testy now. "Did you by any chance make coffee?"

"Hell, no, I don't mind!" Josie shouted. "And yeah, I made coffee. Hurry the hell up."

With that, Evie watched her dearest friend sweep from the room, slamming the door as she went.

* * * *

"Stop right there, running boy!" Josie. Shit.

"Hi, Josie!" Gibb managed a fake smile. "How was the trip down?"

Eyes narrowed, Josie glared at Gibb, obviously not buying what he was selling.

"Uh, huh," she grumbled, nodding. "So *that's* how we're gonna play this, huh?"

"I don't follow?" Gibb returned uneasily. Josie was acting a little funny and he wasn't at all sure he wanted to know what her problem was.

"Just have yourself a little seat and I'll pour you a cup of this nice coffee," Josie smiled sweetly. Sweet like a hungry barracuda. On the heels of her aggression just moments ago, Gibb was becoming more and more uncomfortable, so he quickly settled himself on a padded stool across the counter from her. "This cup right here?" She held up a rosy, pink hued mug. "This is Evie's cup. And look, here she comes now!"

Indeed, there she was. As always, Evie looked lovely, though she'd done little more this morning than shower quickly and pull on a light, casual dress.

"Coffee," Evie groaned, pulling her steaming cup of brew close and lifting it carefully. "Morning, Gibb." She smiled over the lip of the mug.

"Evie," he greeted her, dropping a wink as he lifted his own mug.

"Is that all she gets?" Josie gasped, outraged. "Oh, come on! You can do better than that!"

With a heavy sigh, Gibb carefully lowered his mug to the counter, lifting a brow at Evie. She put her own coffee down and leaned toward him, placing a nervous palm on his shoulder. Gibb leaned over and kissed her affectionately on the cheek.

Josie growled deep in her throat. "Don't *even*," she snapped.

It was obvious that Josie had come into information that Gibb didn't know about. There was no reason to play it coy in that case. Gibb looked into Evie's eyes and shrugged. Evie smiled and shrugged back, leaning forward to kiss the side of Gibb's mouth. Lips curving in a helpless grin, he scooted forward, pulling her off the stool and against him, into the vee between his legs.

His arms went around her, her hands gripping his biceps as she moved to kiss the other corner of his mouth. He caught her face between his palms, tilting her head so that he could nip at her lower lip, nibbling and then licking until her eyes closed and her mouth opened. He covered her mouth with his own, dipping his tongue inside, sweeping her mouth, exploring, tasting the sweet, full flavor of toothpaste, coffee and Evie, drunk on the taste, hungry for more.

One leg hooked around her calf as his hands slid down to cup her wonderfully rounded rear-end. At the same time, her hands slid up his arms, wrapping around his neck.

"Hey! Hey now!"

A solid *thunk, thunk* got his attention and he slowly, reluctantly pulled away, dipping in for one more brief taste, and then another.

"What is *with* you two?" Josie screeched, clearly appalled. "Do I have to hose you down?"

Ever the gentleman, Gibb carefully helped Evie climb back onto her stool, handing her the cup of coffee she'd been drinking. "You're the one who said we could do better than that. Well, you were right," he smirked.

"You already know we slept together last night, Josie. What else do you want to know?" Evie asked.

"I want to know if two of my best friends ever are suddenly...have suddenly..." Josie floundered for a moment before sitting heavily on a stool on the other side of the counter. "If this means in any way that you've lost a hundred and sixty pounds of unsightly tumor—namely Ritchie, then I don't mind a bit! I'll even bring you breakfast in bed next time. Look. Neither one of you are the type to indulge in extramarital affairs. You've known each other forever. What's going on?"

Evie chewed delicately on her lower lip, considering Josie at length. "My lawyer says that since we've both signed on the dotted line, my marriage is pretty much over. But I have to show up in court before Ritchie and I are officially divorced."

"Oh, thank god!" Josie breathed. Turning to Gibb she sighed, "I've never liked Ritchie. I tried—but what can I say? He's an ass."

"I, uh, I didn't like him either," Gibb shrugged. What else could he say? It was true; Ritchie was a twit, no two ways about it.

"Dora was likable, Gibb. Where is she? What's going on there? Is she back in?" It was common knowledge throughout their tight-knit group. Dora had problems. "I don't want to judge, but..."

Gibb looked at Josie uneasily and then over at Evie. Evie arched a dark brow at him.

"Hey, I told," Evie murmured under her breath.

"Not all of it," he whispered back.

"What's wrong with Dora?" Josie asked, her voice rising.

"Dora's back in for bulimia. She's having real problems," Gibb explained.

"And that led you to…"

Gibb had to cut her off before she said something they both regretted. "She filed for a divorce before she went back in, Josie," he told her quietly. "I guess she decided that sticking with her old habits is easier than being married to me." He stood and turned away, running a hand through his hair and pulling several long strands free. "Shit!" he growled, sitting back down. "I know that's not fair. We haven't really worked out why she wants a divorce or even how I feel about it. I know her illness is completely separate from our relationship—even though it impacts it. I mean, of course it does…"

Josie slumped disconsolately onto her stool, forearms resting on the counter as she hung her head. "I'm sorry, Gibb." She turned to look at Evie. "I'm sorry about Ritchie, too. I know you loved him."

Evie reached over and squeezed Josie's hand. "I don't know how I feel about Ritchie anymore. It's been a long time since I've really loved him like a woman should love her husband. Don't worry." She smiled weakly at her longtime friend. "I know you've always had my best interests at heart."

"Honestly, it's true," Josie confirmed, her voice stronger now. "All I've ever wanted was you to be happy. Both of you." She leaned over and gathered the mugs, crossing the kitchen to refill them. "So, what are you guys doing then?" she asked, looking from one to the other.

"Uh, amazing rebound sex?" Gibb offered.

"Incredible good-friend sex?" Evie shrugged.

"You guys are having amazing and incredible sex?" a high-pitched voice squealed from behind. "That is *so* cool!"

"Tricia!" Josie screeched.

"Josie!" Tricia cried, throwing her arms around the taller woman.

With Josie distracted, Gibb ducked out, glancing guiltily back at Evie as he slipped through the kitchen door, pausing before he headed out the front way.

"Weasel!" Evie mouthed as he blew a kiss at her and escaped.

Chapter Four

Tricia went around the counter bar and sat down next to Josie. Lynne, Tricia's partner, took the stool that Gibb had vacated.

"Sooo," Tricia began, looking innocently at the ceiling. "Gibb and Evie finally caved, huh?"

"What do you *mean?*" Josie demanded.

Before Tricia could answer Josie, Lynne turned to Evie. "Sometimes when I'm watching *Life's Blood*," she said in a low voice, talking about the TV show that Evie co-starred in, "sometimes it hits me that Michaela is really you. It just blows me away."

Evie was more than happy to talk about her work and not her sex life for a change—well, sex event, because up till now, she hadn't had a sex life to speak of in a year or more. "Sometimes I'll hear about a video game and realize that Tricia designed it. Or come across one of Erick or Lani's pictures. I know what you mean," she smiled back.

"Oh, go ahead and say it," Josie ordered. "You'll see a movie and realize Gibb wrote it. You're not getting out of this conversation that easily."

Evie sighed and shook her head. "Josie, let up. I'm not going to talk about it right now. I *will* however, talk about what happens when Dragos rescues Michaela from the evil, seer-sacrificing sect at the beginning of next season. Of course… I can only tell you a little bit. I don't want to ruin it for you."

"Oh, no, don't even tease!" Lynne gasped. "You can't possibly ruin it for me. I *need* to know if they get together!"

Evie had opened her mouth to reply when Josie's husband Luke, answered from the doorway. "If you believe what you read in the paper they do!" he announced, holding up the entertainment section of the morning paper. "Maybe not the same two you're talking about, but Evie's one of 'em."

Evie plopped down hard, eyes fixed on the very clear picture of Gibb leaning across the table, his lips touching hers, both their eyes closed. Even if their faces hadn't been clear in the picture, the caption explained it all.

Screenwriter Gilbert Weston and Actress Eve St. John—Apparent longtime friends and recently divorced from their respective spouses. Wedding bells? Or a torrid affair?

The article went on to speculate the length and breadth of the alleged affair, and whether or not the divorces were the result of same. The well-informed journalist was very thorough—pointing out the fact that Eve had never been in a Weston written television show or movie and wasn't signed to appear in any.

Evie shook her head in disgust as she read the article. Ritchie was the main source of information for this newsy little piece and it was obvious that he was bitter. What he had to be bitter about, she had no idea. After all, he had asked for the divorce and he was receiving a handsome alimony to boot.

That isn't to say that she didn't want the divorce herself. Oh no. Not only did she want the divorce, she was more than happy to pay for it. Still, it aggravated her that he had seized the opportunity to broadcast their differences so publicly. Yes, the tagline clearly identified the article as an Associated Press story. It was everywhere.

Even as she considered the situation, she could hear her cell phone ringing upstairs. If it was Ritchie...no, she wouldn't talk to him. He'd been restrained in court from using her public image as a means to promote himself. Maybe her first phone conversation this morning should be with her lawyer.

* * * *

"No, Ed," Gibb addressed his public relations agent. "I don't want to make a statement. I kissed a dear friend over a plate of crab cakes. That's not news."

He looked over at Evie who was pacing back and forth across their little section of the back deck. If he tuned into what she was saying, he wouldn't hear what Ed was telling him. At least he knew she wasn't talking to Ritchie. She'd let all of his calls go straight to voicemail.

Regardless, while kissing her in a public place hadn't been news for him, it was for her. She was a reasonably well-known TV personality. Her ex was using that fact to get a few licks in, apparently. The only good thing so far was that Ritchie didn't know anything about Dora. The persistent media, however, were no doubt looking for her. He didn't want to go down that road, but someone would. He was just about to mention that to Ed when Evie moved into his line of sight.

"Gibb, have you got a minute?" She looked tired, frustrated, bite-able. No damned wonder that hulking British oaf seemed to enjoy his job so much. She smelled good too.

25

"Ed, I'll call you back," Gibb murmured into his cell. "Have a seat?" he asked her, waving at the other little wrought iron patio chair next to the glass topped table where he sat.

"Couple-a beers," Josie said, startling them both. "I'm heading down to the beach, but you looked thirsty."

She handed the two long–necked bottles to Gibb with an understanding smile. Evie smiled back as Gibb twisted the cap off of the two bottles, setting one down in front of her.

"Thanks," Evie called after Josie who lifted a hand without turning around, instead jogging down the stairs and into the sand. "I never drink beer unless I'm with Josie," she murmured, tipping the bottle back and enjoying an icy swallow.

"Beer and the beach—mmm, mmm good." Gibb smacked his lips in pleasure. "So, what's up?" It wasn't as if he didn't know. He just wasn't sure which part of this little event she was addressing.

Evie sighed. "I guess *we* are." She aimed a wry smile at him before looking fixedly at her beer bottle, manicured fingernails worrying at the label. "Thousands of people get their end off every day and it's no big deal…we do it once after a decade—*and* two divorces…"

"Um, what?" Gibb arched a cinnamon brow at her. "End off?"

"Uh, shag…screw," she explained, blushing.

He chuckled, shaking his head. "You're spending way too much time with that Brit. Don't they ever say *fuck* like everybody else?"

"They've got a million other ways to say it." She shrugged. "All of them sound like more fun, too."

"What did you and Ritchie call it?" he asked curiously, brow furrowed.

"I really can't remember, it's been so long. He was a whiner and that really didn't put me much in the mood. Uh, right now, though, I think we need to do a bit of damage control. I can't believe anyone would bother taking a picture of us kissing."

Gibb lifted the folded newspaper and spread it out. "It's a good picture," he murmured, looking at it objectively. "That's a good angle. I bet the camera they used cost a grand, easy."

Evie rolled her eyes. "Picture quality notwithstanding, we need to address this. If we don't make some kind of a response the speculation could get out of hand. I mean, I don't think I'm that important per se, but with Ritchie feeding the fire, Dora could get pulled into it."

Gibb tipped back his beer and guzzled it, thinking. Evie had a pad and pen and was writing and crossing things out as she sipped at her beer. As much as he hated letting the public into his private life, she was right.

"Be right back," he mumbled, standing.

He needed to consider this. By virtue of what they did, both he and Evie were public figures. He wasn't quite as public as she was by virtue of not being on TV every week.

Their friends thought it was cool—the idea that people they knew were somewhat famous. They were right; it was cool. Sort of... But it did have its drawbacks. If he spent any time with her at all, his face could become as recognizable as hers. Was that even an issue here? Maybe not this second, though it was certainly something he should keep in mind.

Chapter Five

Gilbert Weston, writer and producer of the popular television mini-series Polymath, and box office hit City Streets, along with Eve St. John, female star of the exciting weekly vampire serial drama, Life's Blood, addressed the rumors building around their recent public kiss. It seems the two rising stars have been close friends for a decade or more and were simply enjoying a bit of downtime at the beach.

Obviously, they remain good friends and fans can expect to see them in public together from time to time.

They kept the statement brief and casual in the hopes that neither Ritchie nor Dora would be asked to comment any further. Now, all that remained was for their respective media handlers to send that paragraph or something like it out on the wires and downplay the story.

Evie stood at the window in her bedroom, pausing in the act of changing for the beach. The sun was already sinking low in the west, painting the sky a stunning fuchsia, bleeding on top into muted violet and white, and trimmed on the bottom by scarlet and yellow. The color of the sea below was impossible to name, but Evie stood staring, drinking it in, remembering why she wanted to be there in the first place.

She didn't know what was going to happen between herself and Gibb—if anything more would. She'd come to Josie's new beach house to enjoy her friends, the company, the camaraderie, the beach. Sand, sun, fun, and peace. The sooner she covered her half-naked body and got outside, the sooner she could get on with the fun.

"Beautiful." Gibb's voice in her ear, breath warm on her neck, took her by surprise. His hands caressed her ribcage before cupping her breasts. "Need a little help with that bikini top?" he murmured.

"Um, Gibb?" Evie stammered. "What are you doing?" Regardless of the question, she pressed the scrap of materiel into one of his hands.

"I'm helping you get dressed, Ev. You *are* coming down to the beach with me aren't you? I don't want to face those people by myself." While he spoke, Gibb straightened out the flimsy straps and triangles that made up the halter top.

"Gibb, you could care less what anyone thinks. Nothing stresses you out."

"Nothing but Josie," he chuckled, pulling the back tie around her.

She couldn't help but laugh with him as she leaned forward, lifting her hair so that he could finish tying her top in place.

"Thank you," she said, feeling a little shy. "Ever the gentleman, huh?"

"I do try," he agreed, pulling her toward him. She did notice, of course, that he was dressed for the water, too. "So, what do you think? Walk me down to the water and maybe meet me back here later tonight? And tomorrow night? And the rest of the week?"

"A beach house affair, huh?" She grinned. "You know…I kind of like the sound of that. A hot, steamy affair…"

"The sand, the sea, the churning surf," he wrapped his arms around her, holding her cheek to cheek. "It's damn near epic."

"Good friends—genial, but platonic when we meet at parties and social events. Except when we're here, at the beach…"

"Here, at the beach our friendship expands to fit…other needs, hmmm?" It wasn't really a question, more of an offer.

Evie's eyes drifted closed when he began to nibble at the curve of her jaw, nipping his way up to her ear. "Only as long as it works…" she added breathlessly. "I mean…" It was hard to think when he sucked on her earlobe like that.

"But of course," Gibb murmured, pulling back to kiss her nose. "We've been friends for a long time. Friends care about each other. I never want to do anything that doesn't work for you, Ev, you know that."

"Same here, Gibb," she told him earnestly, looking into those summer blue eyes that held her still, every time she looked at them.

"I can't promise I won't want to get down to this beach house a little more often, Ev. We'll have to keep that in mind," he warned her.

"You may not want to come down here at all sometimes," she suggested carefully.

His eyes searched hers for long moments until finally, he shook his head slowly.

"That's possible, of course," he shrugged. "I doubt it. But it *could* happen."

"Anything *could* happen." She arched a brow at him. "We aren't trying for a secret affair, are we?"

"No, I think not. We don't appear to be very good at that." He laced their fingers together, tugging her gently toward the door. "I was thinking more of a low-key, old friends kind of thing."

"Okay then, I'm in." She nodded, snagging a thin beach wrap as she slipped her feet into a pair of light sandals.

"Took you guys long enough!" Josie greeted them as they made their way down the sand dune to the beach.

"We thought you were up there working on your *torrid affair*," Luke joked, handing Gibb a beer.

"Thanks, Josie." Evie smiled, taking a chilled bottle from her. Gibb leaned over and twisted the top off with a wink. "We wanted to come down and toast to our affair before we carried on anymore."

"Really?" Tricia asked, looking around at the two of them.

So far, only Tricia, Lynne, Josie, Luke, and Evie and Gibb had arrived. No doubt, the others would have plenty to say about the newspaper articles when they arrived. For now, the fewer, the better.

"Really," Gibb assured her. Raising his bottle and tipping it forward, he said solemnly, "To Gibb and Evie's beach house affair."

Evie lifted her bottle and gently tapped his.

"Why not?" Luke shrugged, tapping his bottle neck against theirs.

"Make love, not war, *ma-aan*!" Tricia crowed happily joining in.

"Works for me." Lynne raised her bottle and touched her bottle to the other four.

"What the hell, have at it!" Josie mock growled, clinking her bottle with everyone else's. "Are we done now? Can we drink a lot and carry on? I'm on a schedule here," Josie demanded.

"Sure," Evie laughed. "I'm done. Let's talk about everyone else's problems and sex life. Sam and Sarah are trying to have another kid, aren't they?"

"Yeah, if they don't kill each other first," Luke grumbled.

"I can't get over how Sam keeps barking at Erick about being gay. Can you say *repressed*?" Tricia observed happily. "He was only slightly nicer to Karl when he came out…"

"Naw, that's just his acerbic personality," Josie countered, taking a healthy swallow from her bottle.

"*That* is just you going through life with blinders on," Luke contradicted her levelly.

Gibb slid an arm around Evie's waist, reaching over for another beer. "Hey, what they do in the privacy of their own home is fine with me. When they bring it here, it's open season."

"That's right." Evie laughed, leaning back against his chest. "Welcome to the beach."

The End

Teacher, Teacher
By JJ Massa

Chapter One

Krayton chuckled as he listened to the exquisite little woman murder a perfectly easy Spanish phrase with her beautiful southern accent.

"Querría un bocadillo asado a la parrilla de queso, por favor. ¿Puedo tener yo los encurtidos en el lado?" she tried to say. The little lady wanted a grilled cheese sandwich with pickles on the side. What she said came out sounding like, *"Querría un bocadillo asado a la parada queso, por favor? Puedo ti en la los encoja dios in el hado?"* meaning: Would want a roasted sandwich to the stop cheese, please. I am able you in the God cripples them in the fate?

Finally, he could take no more and decided to be a hero. He walked to the table where the lovely little flower of the south was becoming more and more frustrated by the second. Even her grumbling in English was becoming very hard to understand.

"I would be honored to salvage this situation for you, miss. A grilled cheese with pickles on the side, right?" She smiled gratefully at him. He did his good deed. Before he could walk back to his own table, she laid a hand on his arm.

"Thank you *so* much, Mistah. I was getting so flustered." Her accent was very pronounced. She gave him an embarrassed smile. "I'm famished, I guess. My brothers say I should never eat on an empty stomach. They tell me hunger just makes me addled."

A man could definitely drown in those sherry-colored eyes. They were so warm. Still, they had a haunted look about them. Suddenly, Krayton didn't want to go back to his table-for-one. He didn't want to be solitary any more. "Think nothing of it, Miss. Mind if I drink my beer with you while you eat that sandwich?"

She looked at him for a minute. He was becoming a little uncomfortable when she smiled. "Please, Mistah, do join me. In fact, I'll have a beer with you." She wrinkled her nose at him, "That is, if you don't mind ordering it for me. Law knows what I'd come away with." He chuckled. This could be fun.

"Please, call me Kray. What do people call you?" He didn't want last names. Okay, sure, he intended to become intimate with this beautiful stranger from the south—that seemed inevitable. Krayton was a commanding man and he generally got what he wanted. But he didn't want a relationship. He just wanted a good roll in the hay.

Her soft voice kept his mind in the bedroom. "I'm Vivian. Pleased ta meetcha," she extended a hand to him. He took it and held it in both of his.

"The pleasure is definitely mine, Vivian."

Kray and Vivian had a couple more beers while they covered what they did and how they grew up. Both were careful not to name cities or even specific states. Krayton worked in a special operations division of detectives in a Northeast city. Vivian was a schoolteacher in the Southeast. She admitted that she was a bit shy.

Krayton Vance was thirty-eight now and his parents and sisters teased him ceaselessly about being single. He liked to keep himself in good shape so he jogged, worked out, helped with community building projects and neighborhood sports for kids. In short, he was very active and well built.

His body was hard and muscular. He had short dark brown hair. His eyes were dark green. He got a lot of comments on them when he turned them on the fairer sex. He liked feminine companionship but he just hadn't found anyone he liked well enough to date steadily.

Krayton acknowledged that he was pretty aggressive. He had two sisters and had never been married.

Vivian had two brothers in law enforcement and was no longer married. Her marriage had been brief and had ended over a year ago.

He loved talking about his parents, his sisters, and their families. She loved talking about her crazy older twin brothers.

Pretty soon, the time for talk was gone. Both seemed to understand that this was a vacation fling. When Spring Break ended and they left Playa de la Rada, they would go back to their lives.

"If we leave here together, Vivian, we'll be going to bed." He looked into her eyes. He wanted no misunderstanding. He could still walk away. So could she. "I want to be clear. I am going to fuck you as many times as I can before our little interlude in Spain is over. Do you understand that?" She nodded. "Say it," he ordered.

"We will–have sex–repeatedly, if we leave here together." She took a deep breath. "Okay, I agree."

He threw some bills down on the table and took her hand.

As they walked along the beach toward their hotel, Krayton stopped and turned Vivian into his arms. He leaned down and placed his lips on hers.

He bit gently on her lower lip and tugged. When she opened her mouth, he invaded it with his tongue. He devoured her mouth with his, intent on taking what he wanted. When he was sure of her surrender, he turned her toward their hotel.

* * * *

They went to her room since it was closer. Once in the door, hunger overtook him. He kissed her face, her neck, and her shoulders. He began unbuttoning her blouse and kissed each patch of newly exposed skin. After brushing her blouse to the floor, Krayton picked her up and carried her to the bed. He lay her down and finished unwrapping his holiday treat.

Vivian slid her hands under his tee shirt. He had such a hard body. The hair on his abdomen leading to his furry chest felt so good to her. He helped her by pulling the shirt over his head and she ran her hands through his chest hair groaning.

She moved her hands to the waist of his shorts but he caught them and pulled them up beside her head.

"I don't have any protection with me, Vivian." Obviously, he didn't want any mishaps. "We'll just have to make do."

She went from flushed with excitement to blushing scarlet. "There's a basket on the night table, see it?" He did. "Reach over and grab it," she directed him. He eagerly complied.

Inside the cellophane wrapped basket was a twenty-four pack of multi-colored, lubricated condoms, a six ounce bottle of AstroGlide®, a can of spermicidal foam, and prescription bottle of – was that penicillin? The note taped to the basket said:

If ya getcha some, we don't want to know a damned thing about it.

L, E & Z

* * * *

Any other time, Krayton would have laughed out loud but he had more important things on his mind.

He tore into the basket and liberated the condoms, then tossed the box on to the bed near Vivian and attacked her luscious body with renewed vigor. With his teeth, he tugged off her bra. He took both her hands in one of his and palmed one of her round breasts. The nipple instantly hardened against his hand. Her other nipple had hardened as well. He sucked as much as he could of that breast into his mouth while pinching and plucking at her other nipple. She was thrashing against the pillow, moaning.

He moved his hands and his body down to her waist, taking her shorts and panties down as he went. He groaned loudly when he got them off. She had a little triangle shaped tuft of dark, curly hair covering the front of her sex but was completely shaved otherwise.

As he stroked, touched, and explored her with his tongue, he finally separated her labia with his hands and buried his tongue deep inside her.

She whimpered and gasped and he felt her passage begin to throb. Inserting a finger, simultaneously, he sucked on her clit, felt the muscles convulse as her cries echoed in the room.

Quickly, he slid his shorts off and moved back up the bed and over her. She looked dazed with the aftermath of her orgasm.

"Taste yourself on me, Vivian." He covered her mouth with his and kissed her deeply. His rod nudged her center and she moved her hand to touch him. She squeezed him and pumped his shaft when he groaned and she took the condom he handed her. "Put it on me, Vivian. Put me inside you."

With trembling hands, she ripped open the little package and rolled it over his thick cock. She took his sheathed staff and guided it to her wet pussy, moving the head up and down on her slit. He reached with both hands and pulled her legs around his waist. Poised at her entrance, he looked into her eyes. His mind screamed, *mine!* Then he plunged.

He thrust into her grinding himself against her soft mound. She arched her back and met his thrusts. She arched again taking him deeper still as he continued to pound himself into her. He felt her channel clench over and over again around him. It was so good it was killing him. Again and again, he thrust into her until he could hold back no longer. He came on a roar, wrapping his arms around her.

They lay there quietly for long minutes. He thought she might have gone to sleep. Vivian dispelled this notion by reaching out with one finger and touching his semi-flaccid cock. He'd removed the condom earlier. The instant she touched it, it sprang to life. He groaned and grabbed her hand. She turned to face him.

"Kray?" She pulled her hand free and began to rub his hip. "When do you leave?"

"In two days. You?" he responded.

"Same here," she said. "You think we can do that again?"

"Mmmm, Baby, don't worry. We're going to do that a lot more before tomorrow night."

Vivian smiled against his chest. She looked up at him, considering.

"What?" he asked. He could tell something devilish was on her mind.

"I know I told you 'bout being a little shy?" She was working up to it. He nodded.

"I really don't have lots of experience." He wondered what she was getting at. *She did say she'd been married, right?* What kind of asexual being could be married to her and let her leave with hardly any experience? "Can I get on top?"

Kray's whole body leaped to attention. He groaned deeply.

"Honey, I beg you to get on top." If this was a sample of her inexperience, he would like nothing better than to broaden her horizons. Why couldn't he have met her sooner? She hid her flaming face against him.

After a minute, she sat up and straddled his thighs. He reached out to touch her beautiful breasts.

She took his hands in hers and pushed them to the mattress, following them down. She began lapping at his chin and stuttered her tongue down his throat. She began to slowly move backwards until she was sucking lightly first on one flat nipple then the other. His penis bumped against her wet center. She scooted back and pulled out another condom.

"What color d'ya think this one is?" she teased. "What if it's pink?" she giggled.

"Honey" he growled, "I'm secure enough in my masculinity; I can survive a pink condom."

"Good," she sighed moving over him. She sank down on him with a moan. It felt so good when he grabbed her and thrust upward.

She pushed against his chest and he released her, falling back against the mattress. Bracing her hands against his chest she began to move up and down on him. It was difficult to maintain a rhythm while he fondled her breasts and massaged the little nub between her legs. Finally, she cried out to him.

"Kray, I need...I want...Kray!" she gasped his name.

"What do you want, Baby?" She shook her head, eyes wide. "This?" he said on a grunt as he thrust upward. "Is this what you're

36

looking for?" e thrust again and once more until she was nodding frantically.

He grabbed her waist and she gripped his hips with her knees as he drove high and hard inside her over and over again. He pulled her mouth down to his and kissed her hard as they came. She clutched tightly at him, her sheath milking him as her body pulsed its orgasm.

The two of them dozed for a while. Sometime later, they showered, pleasuring each other under the hot, stinging spray. There wasn't much talk between them as they tried different positions and learned each other's tastes and touch.

* * * *

Kray could see that Vivian was exhausted but he was loath to let her go. It wouldn't be right, he thought, to declare himself in love with her. All the same, he just wasn't finished with her yet, damn it!

He was trying to decide how soon he could take a trip south when the phone rang. Grumbling, Vivian rolled over and answered it. He listened to the one-sided conversation for a minute.

"'Lo?" She sat up. "I'm awake." Her brow was furrowed now.

"When?" "But my flight…"She shot to her feet, still naked.

"That fool ain't got a lick o sense." She began to pace.

"He's a liar, Ezekiel!" She stomped a bare little foot.

"What time does the trial let out?" and then, "How long I got?" She sank to the floor.

"Suck eggs, Zeke, that ain't no time at all!" She ran a hand through her hair.

"All right," Deep sigh.

"You, too."

"Bye."

She hung up the phone. He heard another sigh.

The best that Kray could tell, some idiot had lied to the caller, Ezekiel–there was a trial and she didn't have much time and was angry. He felt pleased that he'd been able to decipher that much. Who said he couldn't learn another language?

She looked very troubled when she moved back to the bed. In fact, Krayton thought he saw tears in her eyes.

"What's wrong, Baby?" he asked. He had a feeling she wouldn't tell him very much and he wouldn't like any part of what she said next. He was right.

"I've got to go, Kray." She closed her eyes. "I've got to go now. There's a car coming to get me right now." Her chin trembled and she struggled against it.

He moved to sit beside her. Placing an arm over her shoulders, Kray told her, "It sounds like you have your hands full. Give me your number and I'll call you in a week or so, huh?" He'd decided that he'd like to see more of the southern states.

She wrote down her number and he gave her a long kiss. Then he began to dress as she hurriedly packed. It wasn't long before the desk told her that her car was waiting. Kray walked down to the lobby with her and helped her with her bag.

In the lobby, a man in a business suit turned as she approached the door. Kray looked and there was another man standing next to the door. Both men were bulky and muscular with the telltale bulge of a handgun showing near their left arms when they moved. Both men looked American. The first man approached her extending his hand.

"Agent Solaris, ma'am. That's Agent Burns," he indicated the other man who nodded.

"We'll be taking you to the chopper, it's waiting near the soccer fields a few miles away. There'll be a jet later on. Zeke or Zack will call you when you're in the air. Your account here has been settled."

He was all business and no emotion.

Vivian turned to Kray, her face strained. He leaned down and gave her a hard kiss. She was gone.

* * * *

Kray had tried to call her two weeks after they'd both returned home. He got a recording telling him that the number had been disconnected and at the customer's request, there was no forwarding number.

Anger swelled in him. He got on the Internet and found that, while her number had been unlisted, it had been a Georgia phone number. Savannah, Georgia, to be exact. But that's all he could find about her. Every avenue he used to investigate her was blocked. The hotel was singularly uncooperative. Eventually, Kray had to accept that it just wasn't meant to be. Maybe it was best. He'd relegate the woman to that part of his memory that housed the best-damned fuck he ever had.

He convinced himself that he hadn't been falling for her. He reminded himself that she was shy and he was aggressive. They hadn't had time to explore each other's natures that way.

They probably wouldn't have worked out as a couple. Besides, he reminded himself, he didn't want to be a couple, he just wanted to keep having sex with her until he didn't want her so bad anymore.

Vivian, when she could think about it, was devastated that she didn't hear from Krayton. She wished she'd had more time before she'd had to shut her phone off and leave town. She'd told Krayton that she'd been married briefly, she just didn't tell him what a nightmare that marriage had been. As much as she missed Krayton, Vivian was glad that he didn't know anything more about her. She'd taken a chance with a handsome stranger and he'd made her feel so beautiful and so good.

She no longer equated sex with the torture that her ex-husband, Carl, had inflicted on her. She supposed that, had Krayton known about her marriage, that wouldn't have been so bad. She was more grateful that he never knew about the aftermath.

The trial referred to on the phone had been her father's trial. Vivian Talon's father had drugged her and sold her in a business deal. There was some question about the old man's competency to stand trial. In the end, he was sent to prison for kidnapping.

The date of that trial had been moved up. That was why Vivian had had to cut her trip a little short. To begin with, Vivian's brothers were livid about what her father had done to her. Their mother had married that no-good, worthless shyster after their father's death and then up and died herself.

The boys were almost fourteen years older than their sister, but they looked after her as best they could. They'd been away when the old man lost his mind and sold his own flesh and blood. He'd never have had the balls to do such a thing if they'd been around.

Vivian had to testify at the trial but she'd never told her brothers about the details of her brief marriage. True, they'd come and rescued her from her husband's home just as soon as they got word of her marriage.

They didn't really know the details of just what they'd rescued her from. The doctors had been bound by privacy statutes and therefore, couldn't tell the men any specifics about her injuries.

Vivian signed a lot of papers and forms upon returning to Georgia following her interlude in Spain, however. She didn't realize that she'd signed a wavier allowing the federal law enforcement officers to have access to her medical records.

She found out the hard way what she'd signed one evening when her brother Zeke began pounding on her door. She stood paralyzed in her living room as her brother began to drop copies of medical reports and hospital photos onto her coffee table.

Clothing had covered most of the bruises and injuries inflicted by Carl. She'd been very careful to keep her brothers from learning that she'd probably need a hysterectomy and that her husband had burned her and beaten her. Zeke looked stricken when he looked from her to the pictures on her table.

"Tell me, baby doll. What did that bastard do to you?" He grabbed her by the shoulders, "You gotta say or I'm gonna imagine all kinds of worse things." Tears were pouring down his face.

"Zeke, It's all over now. It's been more than a year, nearly two," she told him. "Honey, please. You saved me, it's all over, Zeke."

"I let you down, baby doll. I wasn't here for you. I love you so much."

Her enormous, muscle bound, tough-guy, federal agent brother was sitting on her coffee table sobbing as if his heart was broken.

"You were our precious treasure and I let that monster hurt you. I'm so sorry, baby doll. I'll never let such a thing happen again. I'm so sorry."

Her brother hugged her until she thought her ribs would crack. He kissed her face and hair. Then, swearing vengeance, he was gone. She'd called her other brother, Zack, but he was too late. A beaten man came to her door a couple of hours later. Zack came to tell her that Zeke had gone to Carl, her ex, and shot him. Carl had been armed at the time and had drawn his gun when Zeke showed up. Carl had pulled the trigger a second after Zeke had pulled his. Both men were dead.

She'd become violently ill. Brother and sister clung together throughout the rest of the trial and the melee that had followed.

Carl Mason had been part of a close but dysfunctional family. Some said the Masons represented the "Southern Mafia". Either way, they didn't like to lose and revenge was a concept they believed in. Carl had married Vivian and therefore, she was Mason property. They were determined to get her back. For herself, Vivian couldn't imagine why. If it had to do with inheritance that would be tied up for quite a while and Vivian wanted no part of it anyway.

For whatever reason, Zack, in agreement with other federal agents, determined that Vivian had to move. Her last name was changed to Talon, her mother's maiden name, and she was shipped up north. She began the school year in a new city, a new state, and all by herself. Maybe it was just as well. Six months had gone by since her Spring Break fling with Krayton.

* * * *

Four months after her move and ten months after that fateful spring break, Special Operations Lead Detective: School Drug, Gang, and Violence Unit, Krayton Vance stared at the closed circuit monitor in his office with a wrinkled brow. He'd turned the volume up a little in hopes that the woman on the screen would say something so he could identify her.

She had her back to the camera and was alone on a ladder in the front foyer putting up a bulletin board, so she wasn't likely to speak any time soon. Bud Lewis, the school's principal, walked in and spoke to him.

"Afternoon, Vance! What's going on?" Bud was a cheerful man.

"Who is that woman, Bud? I don't recognize her." Krayton still stared at the monitor.

Bud chortled. "That's Ms. Talon. You've seen her, haven't you? She doesn't mingle much."

Krayton had seen her but he didn't remember her having such an attractive figure. In fact, even this morning when they'd passed in the hall, she'd looked downright shapeless.

Now, she seemed to be wearing a figure-hugging dark red sweater dress—hugging a very curvy figure—with black tights covering very nice legs. She'd kicked her shoes off before climbing the ladder.

"You mean English-Lit-and-World-History, Ms. Talon? Are you sure?" She worked in the advanced classes where there was less violence, but still, he would've remembered curves like that.

While he was still trying to puzzle it out, Krayton saw a man enter through the front doors. He was a very large, muscular man of about forty with steel-gray hair and permanent laugh lines bracketing his eyes. He had the stamp of authority about him and a bulge on the left side of his chest to go with it.

Kray's sisters would no doubt think he was sexy and hot. Krayton knew he was law enforcement and wondered what he wanted here.

The man whistled roguishly and said to Ms. Talon's back, "Mm, mm, mmmm! Look at that fine ass. You must be a Southern woman, 'cause I know they don't make nuthin' that hot up here."

The woman curved one shoeless foot around the other calf and slid down the ladder, whipping around with a wide smile. The man let out a little high-pitched scream and jerked his gun out from under his coat.

"Stop right there, lady! Arms at your sides," he rumbled harshly, pointing the gun at her.

Her eyes went round and she said, "Zack?" Something about her voice had Krayton leaning closer to the monitor. The woman had dark brown hair cinched tightly at the back of her neck. She wore thick black glasses and no makeup.

The man held up one hand, palm out and told her, "Not one word until you surrender your weapons!"

Huffing, the woman growled, "Zack!" to no avail. With his thumb, the man she'd called Zack pulled back the hammer on his gun and took one step forward.

"Shouldn't you do something? I think the police should get involved, don't you?" asked Bud nervously.

"I think that *is* the police, Bud," Kray answered. "Let's just see what happens." He was riveted to the screen.

Rolling her eyes, she leaned forward, keeping her arms loosely at her sides. Still holding the gun on her, Zack reached out and plucked the glasses from her face. He crushed them in one hand and tossed them toward the trashcan.

Still training the gun on her, he gave her a curt nod. With a deep, long-suffering sigh, she took a step forward and bowed her head toward him.

Krayton Vance and Bud Lewis watched, fascinated as the man began disassembling the bun at the back of her head. There hadn't been time to get a good look at her face, and the scene unfolding on the screen captivated the two men.

From what they could tell, a lot of hair had been confined in that bun. Ms. Talon reached up with both hands and raked them through rich brown hair and then looked up. To the men watching, it seemed that she looked right at them.

Kray felt like he'd been kicked in the stomach. Where a moment ago the homely Ms. Talon had stood, there was now a little goddess tapping an impatient, shoeless foot. A little goddess he knew intimately. Well, he'd known her Biblically, that's for sure.

Holstering his gun, Zack held both arms wide and grinned, "There's the reason people think southern boys sleep with their sisters! Come here, Sugar Bear!"

With a lopsided grin, Vivian Talon flung herself into the large man's arms. He wrapped both arms around her and buried his face in her hair, twirling her around twice. Slowly, he eased her to her feet but he didn't let go. He raked a hand through her hair and planted a loud kiss on her forehead.

Tilting his head to one side, he tapped his cheek with a finger. She dutifully kissed it. He repeated the process on the other side of his face and so did she.

"You are definitely a sight for sore and sorry eyes, little Sugar Bear," he gruffed. He held her away from him and accused, "Have you lost more weight?" She dipped her head. "Okay, never mind for now, honey. How's life in the frozen north?"

She smiled brightly for a minute and then her chin began to quiver slightly. She tried to look away.

In his office, Krayton Vance inhaled sharply. How was this woman who'd worked right here for four months without catching his attention—how was she ripping his guts out now? How the hell had she gotten here? What was best damned fuck he ever had doing in his school?

He didn't know who that man was but Krayton was interested in everything he could learn about this beautiful woman who'd been hiding right under his nose. Hell, he would have paid more attention to the plain Ms. Talon but she never looked lower or higher than his elbow and avoided any kind of conversation.

He'd always wondered why the kids loved her classes so much. He'd heard a couple of the boys say she was hot but he thought they had been joking.

The giant called Zack turned her head back to him with two fingers under her chin. "C'mon now, Sugar Bear, 'fess up. Are you lonesome for those soft southern breezes? You miss hearing from folks who talk slow enough to understand 'em? Not enough green stuff around here?"

"Yeah, all that, sure. I guess I'm a mite homesick," she said softly.

Krayton noticed how pronounced her southern drawl was now that he was paying attention. Of course, now she was having a more-than-one-word conversation with someone.

Tomorrow, he was definitely monitoring some of her classes.

"Talk to me, honey!" ordered Zack. "I cain't help if I don' know what's at issue here." His southern drawl was becoming even more pronounced, too, it seemed. He swept Ms. Talon into his arms and sank down on the floor with his back to the wall. One knee was braced behind her like a cushion.

They still faced the camera mounted in the ceiling. Krayton's blood was boiling. Who the hell was that man with *his* Vivian?

Ms. Talon leaned back against the man's knee. "Ah got a lettah from Carl's family's law-yah," she sniffed. Kray was working hard to decipher what she was saying.

"They gonna sue me for telling Zeke what Carl did to me." She sniffed again. "I didn't tell him, Zack, you know I didn't!" her voice trembled.

"They say it's my fault Zeke killed Carl. Doesn't matter that Carl killed Zeke right back." She took another gulping breath.

Good Lord! Krayton decided he needed to go through her employee folder right away.

"That ain't all, is it, Puddin?" questioned Zack gently. "C'mon," he wheedled. "I brought you a taste o' home. Better get the bad stuff out so we can get on to the good stuff." He lifted a steel colored brow at her.

"You right. There's more." she let out a shuddering breath. "Ah got a letter from Gerald, Carl's brother. It's ugly, Zechariah. It's real ugly."

Zack squeezed her tight and rocked her. Rising with her in his arms, he placed her on her feet and looked intently at her face.

"Sugar, I swear I'll take care of this. It's why the good Lord put me on this earth. Looking out for your sweet ass."

He reached around and gave that sweet ass a loud smack. He grinned at her. Kray wouldn't argue that her ass was sweet, but he didn't think highly of this guy smacking her on it. That was *his* sweet ass.

"Get your stuff together and let's get on out of here. I'm ready to get 'faced."

Apparently, Ms. Talon was ready to get 'faced, too. Still, while gathering up her supplies, she warned the big man that she couldn't have too much excitement.

"Don' forget, Zack, I have work in the morning," she cautioned him.

"How far away do you live?" he questioned.

"Two minutes driving, ten minutes walking I guess," she told him.

"Sugar, we'll be drunk and passed out by ten o'clock tonight even if we eat," he laughed. "And I'll drive you in the morning. We'll leave your car overnight. I don't want you walking."

* * * *

Bud Lewis chuckled as he moved away, and went about his business mumbling, "It's always the quiet ones."

Krayton Vance checked his schedule for the next morning. He checked Vivian Talon's schedule, too.

He somehow didn't think she knew he spent any time at this school. He kept a reasonably low profile and he wasn't here every day. He kept an office, though here since it was the district's largest and most prone to trouble.

Every time he'd seen Ms. Talon, she had her head down and was scurrying to her classroom or her car. He'd never noticed her looking directly at anyone over the age of eighteen. That is, when he noticed her at all.

Wait, he had *heard her speaking to the office secretary.* Kray remembered that because he had thought he'd heard a familiar voice. He'd been so sure it was Vivian and she hadn't been there when he'd looked. Only now, he knew that she had been.

It had been ten months since he'd last seen her and held her. Ten long months he'd missed her. She had some 'splaining to do.

The next morning, Friday, Krayton Vance arrived at the school early. He wanted to keep an ear out for Ms. Talon. She didn't know it, but he was definitely going to keep tabs on her.

He'd start with her employee folder and then he'd monitor a few of her classes. To be fair, he'd look in on some of the other classes in her departments.

As he perused Ms. Vivian Talon's employee record, he was a little surprised. She was twenty-six, which wasn't hard to believe. She looked a bit younger without her "accoutrements" he thought, but still, she seemed mature enough.

He pulled out the background check. It turned out that she had been divorced about three years ago. The interesting thing about that was that she'd been married less than two weeks. Even more interesting was that she had reverted to her maiden name right away. There were some gaping holes in this report. Her next of kin was one

Zechariah Taber of Savannah, Georgia, brother. Brother? Krayton was ecstatic. *Hey, didn't she have twin older brothers?*

Her father, Everett Josephs was living but—could this be right? Her father resided in Georgia's Federal Penitentiary. The story behind that would no doubt be fascinating, especially considering that Zechariah was a Federal Agent.

It looked like she'd had another brother. Ezekiel Taber, deceased. *Wow, it seemed he'd become deceased at the same time that her ex had been killed. Curious-or and curious-or.*

He checked the dates. *Holy Shit. Her brother and her ex-husband had both been killed right after Spring Break last year.* That was about ten months ago, now.

She was five feet and two inches all and weighed one hundred and seven pounds. Brown hair, Brown eyes. She lived almost two miles from the school.

* * * *

When Vivian Talon entered the office to grab her mail, her friend who was the office secretary, Janice, spotted her right away.

"Hey, Viv!" she greeted her. Krayton had been waiting for this. He leaned just inside his door to listen.

"You look a little rough today, Hon." The secretary looked her over carefully.

"Hey, Jan," she grinned impishly at her friend, "I think I hurt myself last night. My brother was visiting," she groaned.

"Hey, what's this?" Vivian asked, holding out a photocopied memo from Krayton. Of course, she didn't *know* it was from Krayton.

"Oh, that's no big deal," Jan reassured her. "Mr. Vance has to pop in sometimes. You know. Don't they do that sort of thing in the South?" she asked curiously. "He's got to keep an eye on things."

"I guess they do." Vivian frowned. "Doesn't say when he'll be along, though." She looked at Janice questioningly.

"Probably didn't want to say and then have something come up. Really, Viv, it's no big deal," Janice smiled. "Bet you won't even know he's there."

Vivian smiled back. "Okay, Jan. No big deal. In a hundred years, who's going to care, anyhow?"

"Wait!" Jan grabbed Vivian. "What happened to those awful glasses you usually wear?"

Vivian laughed out loud. Krayton thought that this must be what tinkling laughter sounded like. He compared it to her sexy laughter when they had played in bed. *Beautiful*.

"My brother didn't like those glasses, neither. He crushed 'em to powder. Guess I'll either get more or just sneak around without 'em," she told Janice.

"You don't wear them in class anyway, right?"

Vivian nodded. "No, I only wore 'em in the hallways. Nobody used to look at me in 'em. Oh well." Vivian waved goodbye to Jan and left.

* * * *

Vivian didn't notice when Krayton snuck into the classroom. In fact, nobody noticed.

The rooms were set up so that a connecting back hall could reach each classroom. It kept the adults from becoming trapped in a sea of students during class changes.

Kray kept himself out of sight so he could see and hear but not be noticed.

The students were working on Shakespeare. In fact, they were conversing and insulting each other in Shakespearean language. They were having a blast and speaking completely in Elizabethan English.

Ms. Talon began the lesson by saying that she'd always enjoyed Elizabethan English, and felt that Middle English was like walking uphill, hip-deep in mud. She preferred the language of Shakespeare's time to that of Chaucer's. She started the ball rolling with a quote From Hamlet, ""My words fly up, my thoughts remain below: Words without thoughts never to heaven go."

Before he knew it, the quotes and explanations for those quotes were flying back and forth. There was much laughter in this class. Now he knew why the students loved her classes. Of course, she *was* pretty hot. He still planned to check on a World History class later.

Everyone left at the end of class laughing and chattering, armed with an assignment to make a conversation out of Elizabethan English relating to a current event.

He had noticed that she no longer wore those awful glasses. He also noticed that her hair was only lightly restrained. In fact, she was wearing clothes that were very flattering.

In the office later, Kray heard one of the men from the Phys Ed department getting to the bottom of the mystery.

"Ms. Talon, has something changed about you? I notice you aren't wearing those glasses anymore. And did you lose about fifty pounds?"

The jerk was being tactless, but she did look one hundred percent different than she had for the last four months.

Her voice sounded strained as she explained, "My brother came to visit yesterday."

She said this as if that told the entire story. A glance showed the other teacher making a questioning gesture so she went on.

"He didn't like the glasses and he took most of my hair stuff and all my baggy clothes this morning when he left."

Kray could tell she was struggling to control her deep southern accent. He chuckled as he heard Vivian still cursing her brother for taking away her camouflage on her way to the lunchroom.

* * * *

She thought she'd be able to zip through the lunch line and eat in her classroom, but luck was not on her side.

Janice noticed her as she paid for her coffee and salad and waylaid her. "Viv, there's this real hunky guy down at the office. He's looking for you!"

Vivian was confused and surprised. She couldn't imagine who it could be. She grabbed her food and followed Janice. Behind them, Krayton followed, too.

A real hunky guy, huh? She was out of her disguise less than six hours and the competition was already lining up.

As she moved toward the office door, she spotted the tall and muscular man standing with his back to her. "Zechariah! I thought you were gone!" She gave him a wide smile.

He turned to her and grinned. "Ah couldn't just steal your clothes and leave, Sugar Bear!" The man was a menace.

"Zack, you're not supposed to call me that at school!" she snapped at him.

He surged forward and wrapped her in a bear hug. "Hush, honey! Those folks are too big to be students. If you don't want me to yell at you for that teaser you're calling your lunch, you'll just give your big brother a great big hug and some sugar to last me the trip."

"I guess I'd better introduce you," she sighed. She was blushing profusely by this time. "Janice, this great big wooly-booger is my big brother, Zechariah Taber."

48

Without taking his arm from around her, Zack stuck out his other hand. "Pleased to meetcha, Ma'am." He smiled at Janice.

Krayton was only too happy to hear that giant declared Vivian's brother, even though he'd already known it was. For some reason, the idea of any other man hugging her or even talking to her, well it just didn't sit well with him at all. He moved to his window and watched as she escorted her brother out to his car. Turning, he called to the secretary.

"Janice! Would you put these notes in the teachers' boxes for me? They're addressed individually. I'll be back in a while."

He handed her a stack of sealed notes and made his way out the door. His pulse was racing. He'd be sitting in front of her in a matter of hours. He was as hard as a rock. He'd go home for lunch and see about a cold shower—a long cold shower.

* * * *

Krayton grinned when he heard Vivian Talon talking to her friend outside his office.

"Janice, do you think I'm in trouble?" she asked the secretary. "He observed my class today, didn't he? Ah never thought there was drugs in my class... Ah bet...oh shoot! I'm as bad as Zeke ever was for worrying," she sighed.

"I thought your brother's name was Zack?" Janice piped up.

Vivian didn't answer. Kray figured he'd save her the distress. He buzzed the secretary.

"He's ready for you, Viv. Don't worry, he won't bite."

Kray just *might* bite the lovely Vivian Talon. Having done it before, he recalled that he liked it.

When she walked in, he was standing at the window with his back to the room. He instructed her to close the door but he kept his voice muffled. He heard the door click and then he turned around to face her.

"Hello, Vivian," was all he said.

She dropped straight to the floor. She didn't utter a sound. He did, though.

"Holy Shit, Vivian! Janice!! I need help!" He scooped her up and moved her to the sofa in his office. Sometimes he'd found it easier to talk to parents or students in a more relaxed atmosphere. Thank God for that sofa.

"Come on, Viv, I'm sorry. Wake up, baby. He tapped her cheeks and loosened her collar. "Vivian, baby, Shit!" He turned to Janice

49

who was looking quizzically at him. "Get me the first aid kit and a wet cloth. Go on!" She didn't move.

"Mr. Vance, do you know Viv outside of school?" She looked at him with narrowed eyes.

"I didn't know she was…just get the first aid kit woman!"

"Do you think I should try to get her brother back here?"

"Not just no, but *hell* no!" he bellowed. "Now go!" Janice scampered away and quickly returned with the first aid kit and a wet cloth.

Krayton snapped open an ammonia capsule and waved it in front of Vivian's nose. She moved her head and waved her hand in front of her face. "Does it hurt anywhere, baby? Did you hit your head?" His voice was deep with concern.

"Ah must've hit it afore I came in here. What in Sam Hill are you doing here, Kray?"

Her voice wasn't very steady, but at least she was making some sense. Just a little anyway. Janice looked on with interest. Neither Vivian nor Krayton noticed her.

"This is my job, Vivian. I'm a detective here." She groaned loudly. "That's how I feel at least half the time, honey," he laughed.

She dropped a forearm over her eyes. He chuckled. He pulled the arm from in front of her eyes. He helped her struggle into a sitting position before he leaned over and kissed her.

"Viv," he said softly. "I didn't realize till this morning…" he took a deep breath, "Well, yesterday was when I realized you were you." He closed his eyes and shook his head.

Janice did her best to remain unnoticed. So far, she was doing fine.

Krayton pulled Vivian into his arms. "Viv, I just found out about your brother, Zeke. I'm so sorry, baby." She wilted against him. He stroked her back. He wasn't offering condolences for the ex.

"It was so awful, Kray." She was working so hard not to cry. "I jus cain't tell you how horrible it was."

He wrapped his arms around her and kissed her head. She rubbed her eyes with the edge of her palms.

"Kray, Ah cain't work with you like this. After my divorce…my ex, he was such a-a cooter!" He arched a questioning brow at her. She shook her head and went on. "He stalked me, beat me, if you know about my Zeke, you know all that. I just wanted some peace and my brother put me in the protection program. Besides, I'm so bad at this romance thing...We cain't date and work together," she tried to explain. "It's just gonna cause trouble."

"Vivian, we've worked together for the last four months without trouble." He gave her a wicked smile. "Of course, you do appeal more without those glasses..."

"Kray, how long you think before one of us gets a hankering for some of that mind bending fraternizing, huh? You don't suppose you'll want to "broaden my horizons" any more? See what colors the rest of those condoms are?" She looked him in the eye.

Janice choked and both heads whipped to her. Poor Vivian had turned an interesting shade of pink tinged with green.

"Janice, that will be all for now, thanks," Krayton declared officiously. Janice grinned. Vivian's head dropped to Kray's chest.

"Vivian, we definitely need to talk. I shouldn't have sprung it on you like this, but we do need to talk. Let me drive you home."

With a deep sigh, Vivian agreed. Kray had had every intention of driving her even if she hadn't agreed. It was late and Vivian had been his last appointment of the day. He sent an inquiring Janice out the door and escorted Vivian to his car.

He'd made note of the address earlier so he didn't need her to tell him where it was.

She wasn't at all surprised. What she remembered of Krayton was that he entered into any given situation knowing what he wanted and from what she could tell, he generally went away successful. Vivian knew she was in trouble. She couldn't even be grateful that it was a different kind of trouble than she'd been experiencing of late. Her life was just way too complicated. And this was one spot of trouble that she couldn't tell her big brother about. At least not yet. She groaned out loud.

Krayton pulled into her driveway and turned to her with a look of alarm on his handsome face.

"Viv? Maybe we should have you checked out at a hospital, huh?"

"Oh, gawd! I'm fine. Just had a bad minute. I'm fine," she declared again.

He took her keys and opened the front door. She moved into the room and looked around, mumbling, "At least Zack cleaned up the whiskey bottles."

Krayton looked at her in surprise but said nothing. The place was nice. It was a small, two-bedroom house with a single bathroom. The layout was simple but she'd polished the wood floors and had been doing some work on the walls. The coverings were textured and simple. He seemed to like it. There was a fireplace in the front room. He didn't know where she kept the TV but it wasn't uppermost in his mind right then.

Vivian was all ready to hit him with her steely determination. She could *not* have a relationship with him right now. Maybe not ever from the looks of things.

Krayton apparently didn't want to hear a word of her steely determination. He silenced her before she could even get started. He pulled her into his arms and lowered his mouth to hers.

Before long, she was lost. She parted her lips, moaning softly. When his tongue caressed hers, his desire was so powerful that she had to hold on for dear life or be swept away.

Without breaking the kiss, Krayton lifted her easily and carried her to the master bedroom. He continued to kiss her as he pulled off her heels and reached for the buttons on her dress.

"Kray," she sighed shaking her head and pushing at him lightly. "We can't do this," she moaned into his mouth. She was struggling to keep from tugging at his shirt and tie. He had just shrugged out of his suit jacket.

"Vivian, there's no way I'm not going to take you now. It's inevitable, baby." He pulled her dress down and moaned at his first glimpse of her breasts. She was wearing a shear, lacy bra, and as he continued to ease the dress off her, the view became more and more heart stopping. She wore lacy, French-cut panties and stockings with garters. She'd told him during their brief affair that true southern belles did not wear panty hose. It was gauche and it was too hot in the south. It was a sight straight from his most detailed of wet dreams.

He put his mouth over one lace covered breast while his other hand cupped her lace-covered sex. He insinuated two fingers under the lace at her thighs and began to stroke her soft folds. She tugged at his shirt and he struggled out of it. With his free hand, he unfastened his suit pants and freed his throbbing cock. Pulling aside the cotton crotch of her panties, he pushed her thighs open wide, leaning forward and rubbing the tip of his cock against her dripping center.

"Tell me again why we can't do this, Vivian?" he groaned as he began to push forward.

"I don't…um, I can't 'member," she gasped.

"Good enough for me," he gritted, plunging deep.

"Krayton!" she screamed, wrapping both legs around him.

Pulling back, he rested just the tip of his cock inside of her, not moving. "Vivian, its time to pay attention," he forced out, his voice harsh and low.

"What're you doing?" She was barely able to speak now, much less focus.

"You want me to make love with you, Vivian?" He remained still, holding her legs open, the tip of his cock just parting her inner labia. He'd never seen anything hotter, forcing himself to look away lest he lose control.

"Uh, yeah, I mean, here I am, legs spread and there you are, you know…" Her voice was high pitched and rising. He was sure she was confused, at the edge of her control, just about overcome with frustration.

He eased forward about two centimeters. "We're gonna date, Vivian, that okay with you?"

"Ah," she moaned. "Right now?" she yelped.

He moved forward one more miniscule bit. "Right now, I'm gonna make love with you. From now on, after that, I want to have you in my life. I want to be part of your life. You think we can do that, Vivian?"

She looked through her spread legs at him, apparently considering. "Sex I can handle, but I don't have good luck in relationships…"

He pulled back a little, fighting his body's urge to plunge again. "We're smart and capable, Viv. How about we try? I'll teach you, you teach me, we'll do this together, starting now, hm?"

"You really want me, Kray?" Her voice was tight, barely a whisper. "A real, long-term, man-woman thing, maybe even…"

"Maybe even for keeps, Vivian…let's try it," he said, waiting still.

"Oh, god, Kray," she moaned. He didn't know what was going through her mind. When she braced herself against the bed, he was certain she'd decided she could do without him. She launched herself forward, wrapping both legs tightly around his waist, and dragging him down, the momentum burying his cock hilt deep inside of her.

"Vivian!" he choked.

"The first thing I'm gonna teach you is not to keep a lady waiting. Fuck me, Krayton Vance, and then we'll go out. Don't tease me anymore."

"Yes, ma'am," he murmured against her mouth, pulling his hips back and burying himself inside her wet heat once again. He took her hips in his hands, pulling her to the edge of the bed. "You ready?" he asked, his heart hammering wildly. Without waiting for a response, he thrust forward, rocking into her, piston-like. Moans and groans, his and hers, echoed around the room as she bucked under him in rhythm.

"Yeah, yeah, I like this, yeah," she panted, her body clenching as she orgasmed around him, over and over.

"Oh, yeah, me, too. I like it, too," he groaned, feeling the heat gather at the base of his spine. "Gonna come, Viv. baby, gonna, gonna," he stuttered and then froze, feeling his balls tighten. "Big, gonna be big."

And then he was coming so hard he thought he'd black out. Vivian's channel clamped tight around him, squeezing him, milking him dry. Somehow, when he collapsed, he managed not to fall directly atop her, but more at an angle. The echo of gasping breaths, groans, and two people recovering from a great deal of exertion resounded around the room for long minutes.

"I missed you, Vivian," Krayton said finally. "I think I love you."

"Really?" Vivian's voice was high again and he turned to look into her beautiful eyes.

"Yeah, really," he assured her.

Her wide mouth turned up in a smile. She sniffed. "Me, too, Krayton. I think I love you, too."

"Good," he said. "That's good."

The End

Dinner for One
By JJ Massa

Maura followed the stuffy maître'd into the dim room populated with sedate diners seated primly at carefully stationed tables covered in flowing white linen. Conversation was hushed, the clatter of silver cutlery against fine china a soft background music as she followed the tuxedo clad gentleman to a small, square table off to the side.

A curt nod from the austere man brought a white-jacketed busboy scuttling up to whisk away the extra chair. "Would Madame care for an aperitif?" the maître'd inquired stiffly, adjusting the tablecloth discreetly to hide the emptiness vacated by the missing chair.

"Please," Maura smiled. She felt the center of attention and wanted nothing more than peace and a lovely glass of wine. "A dry red wine if you will." Sweeping her loose skirt under her, she sat carefully on the padded chair, allowing the gentleman to scoot it in for her.

"Michele," he said and turned to a swarthy young man, Mediterranean, no doubt. "See if you can find a nice Pinot Noir for the lady." Turning back to Maura, the older man promised her, "I shall leave you now in Michele's capable care."

I wish, she thought, her eyes sweeping the sexy young man. Aloud she said, "Thank you, Michele."

With a wicked wink, Michele leaned down to her ear, ostensibly adjusting her chair. "Anything for a beautiful woman."

Maura shook her head with a smile. For those words alone, Michele had earned his tip tonight. She was glad she'd decided to treat herself. The last few months had been hard on her and she was rebuilding her life, finding new places to belong. A place that had such attractive and delusional young men waiting tables certainly had possibilities. *Beautiful. Sure.* She sighed heavily, toying with her fluffy white napkin. She knew she wasn't beautiful. Far from it, in fact. Any illusions she'd had about that were long gone these past three months, thanks to her estranged husband, Frank, and his candid description of her.

Old and fat, he'd called her, just before he'd walked out. The old part didn't bother her, she might be a year or so past forty but he was a year or two older than she was. She'd earned every minute of those years and wasn't at all ashamed of her age. Fat, though? That *did* sting. She was closer to two hundred pounds than one hundred, that was true, but she was healthy. Who didn't have ten or fifteen pounds they'd like to shed, anyway? Apparently, Frank and his new, younger, svelte girlfriend were the perfect size. She sighed heavily.

"Such a sad sigh for a lovely lady." It was Michele, placing her full wineglass in front of her. Had he meant to brush her breast when he placed her wine on the table? "What can I do to please you this evening, hmm?"

She gave him a knowing smile, promising herself that his tip would be a very big one. She didn't believe his foolishness, but it was fun to flirt again.

"What I want isn't on the menu, Michele," Maura grinned, teasing.

"No?" the handsome young man inquired, tilting his head, his swarthy, chiseled features rich and intriguing in the half light, his short black curls bouncing softly.

"Alas, no, so I'll take a fruit and cheese platter if you have it." She was sure her face really did look sad. How she wished that Michele could be hers to enjoy tonight.

"It would be my pleasure, Madame, to provide you with sustenance, but one such as you should never settle for less than her heart's desire."

Before she could respond, Michele was gone. What a sweet young man, she thought. Sweet, hot, hunky…well, she wouldn't be a candidate for his Saturday nights. That was fine. It cost nothing to dream, though. Lost in thought, Maura aimed a distracted smile at him when, minutes later, he placed her light meal in front of her, silently stealing away as the lights dimmed and a stringed instrumental group began to play. The classical music was soothing and just loud enough to make her forget that she had no one seated across from her. Sipping her wine, Maura leaned back in the wide chair, crossing one leg atop the other. A glowing wall sconce behind her cast a dim light over her shoulder and she could see her plate, should she want more to eat from it.

When she felt something brush her calf, she startled, leaning forward to sweep it away. Her hand encountered a linen jacket and she caught her breath, looking under the table into two sparkling obsidian eyes reflecting the gentle light as Michele gently lifted one of her crossed legs off the other and placed both her feet on the floor.

Balanced on his knees, he stroked the tips of his fingers up the backs of her calves, caressing the sides of her thighs and gathering the loose skirt she wore. His eyes focused on her face as one long and elegant finger traced the side seam on her French cut panties, making its way down to the elastic lace at the juncture of pelvis and thigh.

Her hands gripped the edge of the table for dear life, her knuckles white in the dim light. She didn't care that her skirt was pooled in her lap, exposing her ample thighs. Instead, she was just grateful that she'd worn thigh- high stockings. That wicked finger followed the elastic from the top of her hipbone, along her abdomen and between her inner thigh and her pubis. A movement to her left caught her attention and a thrill of fear coursed through her.

What if someone walked up to the table? What if she was caught? She forced a smile and shake of her head at the busboy that glanced her way, proffering a pitcher of water. Her excitement gushed at the near miss and again when the tip of Michele's finger slid under the elastic to stroke the soft fold of her outer labia.

Maura shifted, wanting more contact. "Ah, ah, ahh," Michele murmured, his voice barely audible through the haunting music of the violinist's solo. Distantly, she heard the rasp of a zipper, and then felt the caress of hot flesh against her leg. Any doubt she'd had about his state of arousal vanished in that moment. He was very large and she felt a clawing hunger low in her belly as she greedily eyed what she could see of his glistening cock.

His elegant hands slid forward to hook the elastic of her panties, tugging gently. She lifted her bottom and he pulled them over her hips and off, stuffing them into his pocket with a sinful wink.

Still frozen, Maura started as one of Michele's hands landed on each knee, parting her legs as far as the small space of the chair would allow. With a dissatisfied grunt, he reached behind and under her, cupping a fleshy globe in each hand. Before she could reason out what he had in mind, he pulled her forward to the edge of the chair.

She leaned back against the cushion, unresisting as he spread her legs further now that her position allowed it. Holding one inner thigh with an open palm, she saw him fish in his pocket and come out with a small flashlight. The tablecloth obscured any light from escaping, but she could see him clearly, as he shone the tiny light on her weeping pussy. She knew she should have been horribly self-conscious—and she was. That didn't stop the juice from flowing unchecked as he stroked up one outer lip, around the top, and down the other side.

The tip of his searching finger next traced the source of her cream, sneaking inside and then out. She shifted a little, wanting much, much more. His dusky thick shaft beckoned to her and his finger wasn't doing enough to please her. She shifted again, a small whimper escaping. Michele turned his head, nipped the tender flesh of her thigh and then looked up at her sternly. She understood. *Be still.*

She couldn't bite back a low moan, she needed him to fill her, assuage the ache building in her somehow, and she needed it now. The finger that was just brushing her inner lips came away to cross his lips in the universal message of silence.

"Shhh," he hissed, moving the cream covered finger from his lips to suck it into his mouth. It glistened with saliva as he sucked it off and leaned forward. With one hand, he continued to aim the tiny flashlight while a finger probed between her cheeks to tease at her hole that was exposed to him as she reclined in the chair. She groaned as he breached it just slightly with the tip of his finger, flicking off the small light. Was he holding himself? Working his large cock with one hand while he probed her anus with his finger?

Her breath caught when she felt his full and sensuous lips suck, first on one inner thigh, and then the other. His finger pushed a little further into her puckered opening and his tongue traced her inner labial lips. With a strangled sigh, Maura leaned back in her chair, no longer trying to watch the curly black head bobbing between her legs, just feeling. That devilish tongue plunged deep into her slit, pulling out too quickly only to be replaced by two fingers.

His clever mouth then found her throbbing clit, sucking and nipping. He continued to frig her dripping sheath with one hand while he continued to slide his other finger in and out of her anus, fucking her in two places at once.

Nearly overwhelmed, she felt the stinging zaps of his teeth nipping at her aching hood, while the smooth slide of his fingers in her pussy and the one finger in her other hole stole every thought, every breath. She felt like she was riding the nose of a space shuttle, closer and closer to the pinnacle, a starburst building behind her eyes. Every stroke of his tongue, every slide of those wonderful fingers so deep inside her, she felt the explosion climbing.

He had to know she was near the edge, so close to coming. The juices were pouring around his fingers, lubricating the way for the third finger that continued to glide into her nether hole, a place no one—certainly no man—had ever visited.

Tears had begun to trickle down her face, teeth clamped tight, she knew any moment would find her wanting to scream her culmination.

Suddenly, Michele sucked her clit into his mouth, curling his fingers deep inside toward her pelvis, finding the fabled g-spot. Maura sucked in a deep breath, white light flashing behind her eyes. Michele bit down slightly on her clit and plunged his index finger to the hilt inside the tight flower of her ass. The wave of orgasm crashed over her, slamming her back against the chair as he groaned his own release into her pussy.

How she kept from screaming aloud, Maura would never know. As she came down from the earth shattering experience, she felt Michele planting tender kisses on her sex, her thighs, her knees, as he repositioned her legs and righted her clothing. Once again, she heard the rasp of a zipper as he put himself back together.

She didn't need to look to know that he'd moved out from under the table. It felt decidedly empty. Reaching forward, she snagged the flute of Pinot Noir still barely touched on the table. Her heart rate finally slowed and she placed her empty glass on the table, wondering what the protocol was for facing her waiter after such an event. Did it call for a thirty percent tip as opposed to the standard twenty percent she always gave? A folded leather sleeve slid onto the table near her hand just as the last note of the cello resounded and the lights lifted a little at a time. Diners who'd stayed for the recital clapped softly.

"It isn't often I receive such a generous tip in advance of settling the bill," Michele murmured, dipping a finger into his pocket and displaying a flash of white satin and lace. Her panties.

She tilted her head back to look up at him. "I, ahhh…" she started.

"I hope you'll dine here again, beautiful lady," he grinned mischievously.

"I think this may become one of my favorite places to visit." She smiled back at him. Yes, she did feel like a beautiful lady. Frank was an idiot. She'd be back. She realized that she really appreciated the way that Michele expressed himself.

The End

Anything
By JJ Massa

Chapter One

Andrei Di Claudio heard the sultry, pulsating rhythm of the drum and saxophone before he heard the woman's seductive voice begin crooning. The beat had grabbed his attention. The husky voice singing to his soul kept him listening.

I would do anything
I would give anything
I guess there isn't anything
To bring you to me…

Who was that singing? Where was she? He rose and moved to the French doors that led out to his balcony. Looking out into the endless night, he concentrated, trying to determine how far away she was. Her singing had stopped moments ago and he heard the raucous sound of excited applause. It had to be coming from the local concert arena, which was, coincidentally, one of the properties he owned in Christopher City. While it was several miles away, it would be a simple enough side trip to make.

Satisfied that he had the proper destination in mind, Andrei shrugged into his elegant black jacket and studied his reflection in the mirror. His hard-eyed likeness gazed back, reminding him yet again of one of the many amusing fallacies about his kind. In an effort to explain the fantastic differences between the races, peasants of old had filled gaps in knowledge with their excited imaginations. Those stories now were only exacerbated by so-called modern society.

Yes, Bram Stoker could take a great deal of credit for many of the wild fallacies, though it was the movie industry that truly made matters worse for his ilk. They had created monsters out of a minority of people that nobody understood or sympathized. True enough, some of them *were* monsters, but not all.

Briefly, he thought of his cousins and the man, the *monster*, who had changed them, enslaved them, and tried to own them. It had been their love for each other and their faith in an ultimate good that had saved them.

Unconsciously, Andrei lifted his hand, stroking over the material below the knot of his tie, feeling for the hard, gold crucifix that rested against his sternum. Few people in these modern times believed in Christ's passion on the cross or even that he had lived.

A practicing Catholic still, Andrei attended Mass somewhat regularly. Upon entering sacred ground, he always dipped his fingers in the trough of holy water near the door. Its only effect on him ever had been to leave his skin wet.

No, most people were filled with silly children's stories about vampires, some so outlandish that Andrei had to fear for those who would believe them. Like most enduring tales though, he found just enough truth in them to ensure their telling and retelling over the years.

Pressing one button on his cell phone, Andrei began speaking immediately upon hearing it answered. "Naldo, bring the car around, I wish to go out."

"Sì, *Signore* Di Claudio," Naldo, Andrei's longtime servant answered immediately.

A member of Naldo Bilardo's family had served as personal valet and manservant to Andrei since just before the turn of the last century. Should Naldo fail to marry and produce a son to take up the position, one of his many nephews would follow in his footsteps.

Upon their arrival at the concert arena, Andrei allowed himself to be conducted inside where the administrative offices were. Naldo waited stoically by the door, ever the vigilant chauffeur, bodyguard, and general right-hand man.

Andrei was certain that the owner of the sultry voice he'd heard earlier had gone from the building. Although there was still music coming from the arena, it was not any music that Andrei found appealing.

"Where is the woman whom I heard singing here earlier this evening?" Andrei demanded impatiently of the Assistant General Manager.

"Um," the nervous man stuttered. He was quite surprised to find himself talking to the man who owned the string of Arenas that paid his salary. "You must mean Alexa?" he asked hesitantly.

Struggling mightily with his emerging temper, Andrei smiled coolly. "She sang a song in which the word "Anything" featured heavily," he informed them in his smooth and cultured voice.

"Oh, yeah," a younger man standing in the doorway piped up right away. "Alexa sings *Anything*. It's her latest hit," he enthused, his expression enraptured. "That's my favorite song! I love it!" he gushed, his eyes foggy as he pictured the young lady while she sang.

Skimming his thoughts, Andrei could not clearly make out the woman's features through the filter of the young man's memory and imagination. It didn't matter. He did not like this man's feelings about the woman he was sure was meant for him.

"Where is she now? What is her full name? Will she be back here? Do you have a picture of her?" he rapped, one question after another, staccato.

"Uhmmm," the young man squeaked, tapping Andrei on the shoulder and pointing.

Andrei turned and looked at a larger than life photo of an attractive young woman who had large hazel eyes, elegant cheekbones, a straight, refined nose and a strong but feminine chin. She wore suede boots that stopped at her knees with large cuffs, impossibly tight jeans that lovingly hugged a voluptuously round derriere, and what could have been a folded army blanket chopped short to barely cover her ribs.

If she hadn't been wearing the wool wrap, her long golden brown hair would have shielded her shoulders and breasts. It fell in waves all the way to her waist in an impossibly thick, living curtain. Something about the young woman called to him.

Anything—I would do Anything...He knew that he would do anything to find her–to see her–to have her.

"Where is she?" he asked again, his voice not as steady now, though no one else noticed it.

"She's gone for the evening, umm, gone to her next gig," the Assistant General Manager ventured nervously. "They'll be playing...Randy, where are they next?" he demanded of the enthusiastic young man. "Get Mr. Di Claudio a concert schedule for Alexa–do we have one just for her?" he asked suddenly. "She's been opening for The Yellow Crows this series, but she leaves the arena because she doesn't like their music," the uneasy manager explained.

"I cannot fault her taste," Andrei offered blandly, calm now that he had a name and soon a direction. He wanted to find her *now*, but he'd learned patience over the last two centuries.

The younger man, Randy, began talking to the manager in hushed tones. Andrei moved away, knowing that he'd learn all he needed to know in moments, and letting the two men conduct their business in relative privacy.

"Sir," the nervous man approached him hesitantly. Andrei scanned the man's jumbled thoughts, knowing he wouldn't like what he was about to hear. "She doesn't have a personal concert schedule and I'm not sure if she's opening for The Yellow Crows at their next stop."

Andrei imagined his hands squeezing the inept man's throat until he caused the manager's eyes to bulge and his face to turn purple. Apparently he'd projected those thoughts quite strongly because the other man paled and stumbled backward.

"Suppose you furnish me with a schedule for the crow group then, hmm?" he suggested in a brittle tone; polite, though inside he was snarling. This woman was his and he needed to find her.

That alone was enough for him, but he felt a further degree of urgency. Over two centuries of existence had taught him to obey his instincts. If she attracted him, she would likely attract others like him. Perhaps even the devil that had made him. He needed to find her. As the seconds passed, the urgency increased. Something was very wrong. The certainty grew in him; he had to find her *now*.

"Naldo," he turned to the trusted employee who had remained silent thus far, waiting patiently beside the door, ready for Andrei's next order.

"Yes, *Signore*?" Naldo stepped forward.

"Order my personal automobile to be readied for me." With a curt nod, he turned and followed the other man out.

* * * *

Alexa leaned her forehead against the cool glass of the tour bus's window. Janie, who was one half of her personal staff, kept the little traveling duplex very clean and homey. It felt good to have familiar surroundings everywhere she went. Nearly twenty-five, she supposed that most people would think she was very young. She certainly didn't feel young. She'd been on her own for the last seven and a half years.

Before that time, Alexa had been part of a family of entertainers. She and her two sisters sang and performed together all over the country. That had ended abruptly when Alexa had been offered fame, fortune, and a contract with a major recording company – without her sisters.

Her family had reacted as if she were turning her back on them. Even before the offer had been fully presented, her family accused her of behaving disloyally. Simply by virtue of being chosen, she'd alienated the only people she'd ever loved. The memory of that day still had the power to bring tears to her eyes and she struggled to hold them back.

Her own mother had called her a selfish tramp and her father had charged that she was a user. The irony, the thing that still swamped her with helpless rage was that she'd never even accepted the offer. She'd been tried and convicted without ever opening her mouth.

The stunned executive who'd offered her the deal in front of her parents was still there when they abruptly left her, throwing a suitcase of personal belongings at her feet. Leaning against the bus window, Alexa closed her eyes, remembering.

It had been such a shock. Even that word didn't touch how she'd felt. Everything in her life–everyone she'd ever known–all gone. She was alone. The horrified man who'd remained with her took her back to his company. That had been Lonnie Chambers, now her manager.

The soul-deep hurt and humiliation still had the power to affect her all these years later. Lonnie had helped her hire a lawyer and become emancipated. She made the decision then to drop her last name. Since he had a vested interest in her success, she'd let him take on the job of her manager. She had no family now, or even close friends, just people who worked for her.

"You're sitting there remembering, aren't you little girl?" a sweet voice asked from behind her.

Alexa allowed herself a small smile. "The smartest thing I've ever done was to hire you and Bernie," she murmured, accepting a cup of coffee from the other woman.

"I agree," Janie said smugly, ruining the affect by giggling.

The older woman sank down next to her sipping from a cup of coffee as well. "I know we aren't your family, honey, and I know you miss them sometimes."

Alexa's brow furrowed and she shook her head in denial but Janie continued on. "Alexa, you know that Bernie and I and Mr.

Chambers are the only people you even talk to anymore besides the musicians you work with. It's just not healthy."

She couldn't argue with Janie, she was right. Still, she just didn't want to think about it. There was no place to go to escape the conversation. All she could do was stop it before it became too intense.

"Don't push me, Janie," she said finally. "You don't know how hard it is to let anyone in at all."

"I guess I don't, honey," Janie said after she took a breath. "I just worry," she sighed.

"Thank you for that," Alexa smiled, leaning back against the cushion and watching the miles roll by.

She did appreciate Janie's worry and concern. She always would. If she were honest with herself, she would admit that Janie was much more a family member and friend than she was an employee. She loved Janie and Bernie. It was a hard thing for her to admit but it was true. She was their employer, yes. Nonetheless, she felt genuine affection toward them.

Settling in to listen to Janie's happy chatter, Alexa determined that she would try harder to let the older woman close to her. The couple didn't have children and she knew they considered her their own lost chick. She smiled inwardly. It was a good feeling to be wanted that way. Scary, yes. Good, though.

Chapter Two

Alexa jerked awake as she heard the heavy diesel bus engine cycle down to an idle. She stood and stretched, glancing back to see Janie push the hair off her face as she sat up.

"I think I'll just stretch my legs," she murmured to the older woman.

Janie mumbled something but Alexa simply nodded and headed for the door, pulling a cardigan over her blouse as she went. Bernie nodded to her on her way by as he supervised the filling of the bus's enormous tanks.

It was either very late or very early and she could see the sparkling pinpricks of fading stars against the dark blue velvet of the night sky. The air had a chill bite to it that felt good on her cheeks. Alexa smiled to herself and spread her arms wide, embracing the quiet, broken only by the rumble of the bus's diesel engine.

"Lovely," hissed an eerie thread of sound as a long, thin arm slid around her middle, a claw-like hand sliding into her hair. "*So lovely, I think I'll have you join me, my dear.*"

No doubt, the muted thunder of the bus engine coupled with her pleasure in the autumn night had masked the stranger's arrival but now, was she even hearing his voice? Frozen with fear, his cool lips had pushed away the collar of her shirt and nipped at her throat. But was he speaking?

"I will have you as one of mine. A lovely companion to do my bidding and meet my needs." His voice floated around her, resounding in and out of her thoughts. "*Yess,*" the snake rasp of words echoed in her head as a white-hot jolt began at her jugular and ricocheted throughout her system.

The stunning heat of burning at her throat, weakness in her legs, and then she felt something stealing from her body. Struggling did little good and the rusty taste of blood filled her mouth somehow.

"Noooo," she gurgled weakly, trying to shake him off and swallowing what must be a mouthful of blood.

"*Ohhh, yess!*" the hissing sound reverberated in her head again and she tried to groan, choking on still more rusty liquid.

Her brain, her mind fought furiously against what could only be a rape, an invasion of her veins of her thoughts by whatever this creature was. She needed to get away and she screamed weakly

66

through the blood and the hand that was pumping his life force into her mouth as he held it clamped over her gaping lips.

She wouldn't give up, she determined. She wouldn't! *"Leave me alone! Help!"* she screamed in her mind. But she could feel her body weakening and she was helpless to stop it. Still struggling, though it was doing little good, she would go down fighting.

"Silly girl, you will be mine! You waste your energy for naught. Give in to me!"

"Nooooo!" she moaned in her mind, unable to speak, unable to spit out the thick and warm metallic liquid. Alexa was sure that she had lost.

* * * *

Andrei slid into the leather bucket seat of his Lamborghini Diablo, wasting no time. Fortunately, it had been readied for him and the large V12 engine was purring like a contented lion.

He felt the woman he'd heard singing. Felt her distress, and even felt the evil that tracked her. Still he closed his eyes in a brief moment of appreciation for the completely impractical, but beautiful and masterfully crafted machine that never failed to stir him.

With a curt nod to Naldo, he put the two and a half ton yellow beast in motion. In less than ten seconds his speed was brushing one hundred and sixty kilometers per hour, one hundred miles per hour, he reminded himself. He *was* in America.

Andrei relaxed his body and let his reflexes guide him as he drove toward the woman, the feeling calling to him. Reaching out with his mind, he searched. He knew who was following her. He would always hear and feel the evil thoughts of the creature that had turned him. Now that vile beast was after the woman he knew was meant for him.

Never mind that he'd never met the woman, never spoken to her. That was incidental. He wanted her so of course she would want him as well. Andrei had every confidence that things would work out for them—if only he reached her in time.

"Leave me alone! Help!" he heard her frantic voice screaming in his head. He was closing in on them; he knew he was.

The sick feeling of evil washed over him and he knew he was close, deadly close to his maker. Almost of their own volition, his hands jerked and the powerful car turned into a truck stop parking lot. He was out of the Lamborghini almost before it stopped, drawn like a magnet to the silent and shadowed figures struggling in the darkness.

"You're too late, my boy. Your chosen has become mine. And you have only yourself to blame." Andrei heard the cold hiss of the hated voice in his head. Balfent, the vampire who'd killed him and his cousins and then brought the three of them back to be his slaves. He determinedly ignored the icy whisper as he hurtled himself toward the obscene tangle of dancers.

While the vampire changing into various creatures had turned out to be so much fantasy, he *could* move inhumanly fast. Andrei struck his nemesis mid-chest, like a linebacker careening across the line of scrimmage, and taking Balfent down like a luckless quarterback.

He was vaguely aware of the woman's weak and strangled scream as he rolled away from her clutching the evil vampire around the middle. Balfent, weak from pouring his own blood down the throat of the woman, used his last strength to throw Andrei off him. In the blink of an eye, he was gone.

A mortal man's strength was still no match for a weak vampire, much less an ancient and powerful being like Balfent. Andrei hit the side of the bus full on. He bounced off, landing on his knees only a few feet from the near-hysterical woman.

"I'm sorry," he whispered as he cradled her, *"So sorry,"* he thought to her as he sunk his sharp fangs into the torn flesh of her throat. *"This will be different next time, I swear it,"* he promised her, drinking only enough to have her within him.

He wished he had time to replace the poisonous life's blood that Balfent had fed her with his own essence but he heard stirring and raised voices. He'd expected a response to his involuntary body-slam and wasn't disappointed.

"Wha-?" the young woman moaned, barely stirring.

"I'll find you again, cara," he sent his warm thoughts to her as he gently laid her on the rocky, oily pavement.

Faster than the human eye could perceive, he was back in his powerful car and on the road, pushing the gas pedal to the mat and away in seconds.

Chapter Three

Alexa woke, feeling as if she'd been wrapped in cotton wool. Carefully she attempted to turn her head, only to discover that her throat had been bandaged with thick gauze pads.

"Shh, sweetie," came Janie's soothing maternal voice. "Don't move, honey, you were attacked." Janie moved out of Alexa's line of vision with a final stroke to the forehead. "Bernie!" she called out. "Get the doctor! She's awake!"

Alexa heard movement and stirred, lifting a hand toward her neck that Janie caught before it got very far. "What happened?" she rasped, her throat felt like a desert dry place packed with sand.

"Young lady, you gave us all quite a scare!" the jovial voice was coming from either a male nurse or a doctor. "I'm Dr. Roston, Alexa," he boomed. Well, that answered that question. "Some sicko with a vampire fetish bit you or cut you…well, punctured your throat really and somehow took some of your blood. Very ingenious, really," he mused, distracted.

For a moment, she wondered if he had a reluctant admiration for her attacker. She didn't really want to think about it but she was sure there had been two. One bad and one… well, she didn't know. What she did know was that both men had bitten her and both drank from her. This was no fetish.

Her thoughts skittered away from her trauma and back to the jovial doctor. She didn't speak but stared at him for long seconds, waiting to see what he would say or do next. He graced her with a plastic smile and leaned over her.

She unsuccessfully tried to pull back as he pried open one eyelid and then its mate announcing, "Well, your eyes look clear. We had to infuse you twice, Missy. You lost quite a little blood. And it seems that your attacker decided you should drink some blood while you were at it. We were quite concerned about typhus and other diseases transferred through ingestion… Don't worry young lady, you've tested clean for that."

"Um," she cleared her throat. "Um, thank you," she forced out. "How long will I need to be here?" she asked.

"What is it with people and this place?" He turned to Bernie and Janie, "Isn't this a nice enough hospital?" His false cheeriness was grating on Alexa's nerves now. He settled a smarmy smile on her.

"Well, my dear, you can leave as soon as your paperwork is all complete. Your tests are negative but I recommend against any performing for a few days, possibly longer. Do you have a personal physician?"

While the last statement was more an afterthought she was sure, she answered it anyway. "I'll go straight to the doctor when we hit Columbia." She smiled, the twitch of her lips felt almost painful.

"Lovely, just lovely. Well, you've tested negative for any creepies and crawlies so we'll just see you on your way then, hmmm?" And with that, Dr. Roston and his fake smile and jovial platitudes made their way out the door.

"Alexa." Janie sounded a little nervous. "Don't you think we should just stop for a bit? You've been injured, honey."

"I'll be fine, Janie," Alexa assured her. "Bernie, I think we *should* stay at a local hotel tonight. Could you take care of that, please?"

She made it a request but they all understood it was an order. Alexa knew the couple wouldn't abandon her. The fact remained, however; they were her employees.

* * * *

Bernie settled them into a small suite at an upscale hotel. Alexa cared little either way about where they spent the night. Really, she just needed to be alone to gather her thoughts. Left alone – but not all alone.

She didn't want to admit it, but she was afraid to be by herself. The incident in the parking lot had frightened her very much. Almost asleep, Alexa nearly jumped out of her skin when she heard the voice echo in her mind. *"Don't worry, Little Lovely, you'll never be alone again,"* came the familiar hiss.

The man who'd attacked her! She jumped up, throwing the comforter to the floor. "Bernie!" she called out. "Janie! He's here, look, I heard him!"

As the older couple scrambled to answer her panicked cries, she heard the reptilian rasp; *"I'm with you in spirit, Lovely, not in body. You're safe for now… but I'm with you…"*

Terrified to her core, Alexa sunk to her knees by the bed, shaking her head in denial. He was there! He was in her head! She buried her face in her hands, fearing for her sanity. Bernie searched the small suite as Janie fussed. Of course he found nothing. Nobody was there.

Finally, Bernie and Janie accepted her word that she would be fine and returned to their room on the other side of the suite. Alexa wrapped a thick robe around her shivering body and found her way to the small balcony. As she looked out over the lights of the strange city, her hand wandered to the bandage at her throat, lightly skimming it with the pads of her fingers.

The wound was still tender to the touch and she focused her mind, not on the disgusting, offensive beast that had attacked her. Not on the man that would hurt her and make her submit to him. Instead, she tried to remember the other man, the one who'd saved her.

She moved to a padded chair and sunk into it. In spite of the events of–had it been only hours? In spite of the events of the early morning hours the day before, Alexa enjoyed the soft silky air caressing her face.

Imagining it was the second man, her savior, she closed her eyes, trying to see him. He'd been dark, swarthy. Was he black–African American? No…She recalled the wash of starlight reflecting a lighter tone. But his eyes, they'd been dark and deep, she remembered that.

What else, she thought to herself as she relaxed more deeply into the cushions. He'd been clean-shaven with silky dark hair. His lips, though…those soft, full lips had skated across her cheek as he apologized, sinking his own teeth into her wound. She hadn't felt the bite, only his lips, working, gliding over and on her skin.

* * * *

The fight wasn't much as fights go. Under normal circumstances, Andrei wouldn't even call the little scuffle a fight. Yes, under normal circumstances. But nothing about dealing with Balfent could ever be considered normal. Nor could finding the woman he was sure was meant for him be considered normal. Put them together and circumstances were anything—everything besides normal.

He'd been slightly weakened simply by being in the presence of the older, more powerful vampire. Fighting the call of his maker had always been a chore; he was at his strongest when his cousins were nearby. The three of them together had been able to break the ancient creature's thrall. Alone, they were nearly powerless against him.

Andrei knew that the combination of surprise and blood loss had stolen the devil's strength and now, the woman, Alexa, would be hearing from the old one. That was the reason why his yellow Lamborghini Diablo was parked down the street from a college bar.

He needed his nutrients, and if he wasn't mistaken, he'd just snared a meal.

A fit young man was bent at the waist, hand shielding his eyes as he tried to peer into the car. The reflection the streetlight cast on the window made it hard to see the interior very well.

"How *you* doin'?" Andrei came up behind the man, mimicking the famous character from a popular TV show. He slid his hand up the younger man's back and rested it at the base of his neck, stroking the soft skin above the collar with one finger.

"Ahhh," the young college student jumped, surprised. "Um, hi," he mumbled. "Uh, sorry mister, I mean, I was just…"

Andrei smiled into the nervous young man's eyes, mesmerizing him. "You wanted to see the car?" He nodded as he spoke.

"Oh, wow, yeah!" agreed the exuberant youth. "My little brother's eighteen and we both love this car! Yellow! Wait till I tell him!"

He couldn't stop a smile as he opened the long, smooth door. "Go on, have a seat," Andrei offered waving his hand to indicate the leather bucket seat. Wide, disbelieving eyes fixed on his face. "Please," he urged, his voice a silky purr.

The young man expelled a sigh as he slid in under the wheel. Reaching in, Andrei lowered the steering wheel and adjusted the seatbelts, effectively pinning the young man in place. Lowering the door into place with a solid *thunk*, Andrei rounded the car and sat down in the passenger seat.

"Do you…" the young man turned toward him. He looked very nervous. "Do you think I can drive it?" his voice cracked in his excitement.

Lifting a hand to the other man's cheek, Andrei caressed his face looking deeply into his eyes. He concentrated hard on the youth, capturing him with his eyes. "You are driving it, Scott," he informed. He leaned closer, his fingers brushing down the throat, tracing his companion's jugular. Rubbing cheek against cheek, he murmured, "Lean to the left, Scott, take that curve."

Scott leaned as if he were taking a long curve in a fast car. Andrei leaned across him and trailed his lips over the throbbing artery. "This is so cool," Scott mumbled, awe in his voice. "Oh, yeah," he whispered, squirming in the low seat, angling to give Andrei better access.

"Yeah," Andrei agreed, his tongue tracing the pounding pulse. He cupped the other man's head as his teeth sunk deep. *Yeah*...he thought as he drank slowly, careful to keep the illusion of a hot ride fixed firmly in the younger man's mind.

As he savored the rich blood warming his mouth, his body, he felt the soothing comfort of--she was thinking of him, he realized with a start, and fought against reacting. He didn't want to injure the young man by jerking his fangs across the tender skin of his throat.

She was thinking of him, taking comfort in him. If his mouth hadn't been full, Andrei would have smiled. The tasty young treat he was dining on murmured to himself again, groaning with pleasure.

Andrei pictured Alexa, concentrated on her. He could feel the air around her. He could feel that she was outside in the cool air. She was allowing thoughts of him to console her and that was a gift for which Andrei was more than grateful. She would make it; he knew it, if only he could keep her safe from Balfent.

Chapter Four

Do you need me?
Anything, Baby
Don't you see me?
Anything, Anything to be
Everything you need
I'll be everything maybe
Anything, you'll see

The saxophone pulsed in the background but Andrei had his attention fixed solely on her. *Sing to me, only to me*, he compelled her. It seemed she was. He stared at her from the owner's box and she appeared to be looking across the crowd straight at him.

She stirred a hunger in him he hadn't felt in decades, more than one hundred years, he was sure. He wanted her and he would have her.

She'd been on stage for an hour now and this was her final song. He knew she was tired. He had heard the raspy voice of Balfent slither through her thoughts as she fought to maintain her composure and perform her song.

She wore a long sleeved, ankle-length dress that clung and caressed her curves. Soon, he determined, he would learn each and every one of those curves and she would know that she belonged to him.

He could hear her heartbeat as he listened to her sing. He knew she was exhausted. She was undernourished as well. He would give her a minute to have a drink of water and then he would visit her dressing room. Patience was a virtue—a virtue he quite resented at the present time but one he would practice just the same.

I would do anything
I would give anything
I guess there isn't anything
To bring you to me...

Her head bowed and the saxophone finished its haunting refrain. Lifting her face, she smiled at the clapping crowd. "Thank you so much for coming to hear me tonight, ladies and gentlemen. Thank you!" She bowed once at the waist, rose and turned, handing the microphone to the announcer who came to hold the crowd long enough for her to get off-stage.

He waited ten minutes and then made his way to the back of the enormous building to her dressing room. The door was opened by a muscular, medium-sized man in his mid fifties. Although reluctant, he stepped back after Andrei introduced himself and allowed him to enter.

"Miss...Alexa?" Andrei asked, taking in the scene.

Alexa sat, huddled on a small sofa while a slightly older woman, perhaps the muscle man's wife, murmured to her, offering a bottle of water.

Andrei extended his left hand to the woman and gently took the water from her. He moved across the dressing room/suite and found a crystal tumbler, filling it with the water. He knew what she really needed. She lived in limbo now. He would help her.

He sat down next to Alexa and pulled out one of her hands, wrapping it around the glass. Helping her to support it, he guided it to her mouth and tipped it. She brought her other hand forward and cupped them both around the glass, drinking thirstily. The other woman beamed at him and stepped away to talk quietly with the man.

"You were out there so long in that heavy dress, *cara*," he murmured, filling her glass again, placing the empty bottle on a nearby table. "Tomorrow you will wear something lighter—perhaps linen so that you do not get so hot," he decreed, eying her boots and the heavy, clinging dress distastefully.

She looked at him as if she didn't understand a word he said. "I'm sure we can come up with something better," the older woman agreed.

He flashed the accommodating woman, Janie, he read from the man's thoughts, a smile, returning his attention to Alexa. "I am Andrei Di Claudio, Alexa." He smiled fully at her as he leaned forward and slipped first one boot off and then the other. "You will come to know me well."

Her feet were so dainty and delicate. He didn't think he'd ever seen such attractive feet before. He rubbed one with both hands as he spoke again, "I own most of the arenas and clubs where you are scheduled to perform. It is quite a coincidence since I first heard you sing this week."

Apparently, she was beginning to cool off because she gently tugged her stocking clad feet away from him and tucked them under her. "I'm pleased to meet you, Mr. Di Claudio," she said stiffly. "Um, thank you for the water and the…" her face colored brightly. "Thank you for the foot-rub," she blushed and turned her head to the side briefly.

He couldn't control a laugh. She was so enchanting in her embarrassment and trying so hard to remain aloof from him. That, he wouldn't allow. He leaned forward and took her hand.

"You are most welcome, *cara mia*," he smiled, tugging her to her feet. "I'm sure you'll feel like a new woman if you have a chance to rest, hmm?"

"I…yes, I suppose I might," she said hesitantly.

Scanning her thoughts, he could tell that he confused her. It seemed that she wasn't used to being touched and that pleased him a great deal. She was meant for him and no one else. He liked knowing that his would be the first intimate touch she knew. "Will you join me for dinner, Alexa?" he asked her as she moved away from him.

"Um, I—really, thank you, but…" she mumbled something he couldn't hear.

Andrei was surprised how awkward she acted at being asked to dine with him. Focusing on her nervous thoughts told him that she seldom received requests for dates. It seemed her chilly façade was effective in keeping people at arms length. People maybe. Not vampires. Certainly not him.

"Please, allow me to escort you to your suite and we will enjoy a light snack. There is a little known passageway leading to the basement of your hotel next door. My manservant, Naldo, will help you," he smiled at Bernie, "with any luggage you may still need to bring up or any other accommodations—perhaps an automobile?"

Naldo, who had been standing quietly near the door as was his habit, stepped forward to greet Bernie.

"Yes, thank you, Mr. Di Claudio," Janie piped up. "Isn't that a wonderful offer, Alexa?" she gushed to the silent young woman.

Warily, Alexa sat back down on the little sofa and Andrei joined her, handing her the boots again. "Um, I guess that would be okay," she gave in finally.

* * * *

Goosebumps chased up Alexa's spine when Andrei's palm settled at the small of her back. When he leaned in close to lead her down the corridor and around a gathering of people, it was all she could do not to press herself against him.

He smelled so good and something about him, some nameless magnetism, affected her in a way she'd never before experienced. Did she really want to get away from him or did she want to move in closer?

As if he knew what she was thinking, Andrei stepped next to her in the elevator so that her hip brushed the top of his thigh. It was a small space and she supposed five people did create very close quarters.

Upon arriving at her door, the only other penthouse in the hotel besides his own, it turned out, Andrei tapped a number on a keypad causing the door to open. He murmured the number in her ear as he did it but she knew she'd never be able to repeat it should he ask.

"I'll be right back," she mumbled as soon as the small party had assembled itself. Janie followed her into her room.

"He's handsome, isn't he, honey?" Janie giggled, pulling out a loose pair of silk lounge pants and top. They were a very stylish dark red with a v-neck and long sleeves.

"I can't wear my pajamas out there, Janie!" Alexa gasped. "I don't even know that man!"

"Don't be ridiculous, Alexa," Janie chuckled. "They're much less revealing than that dress you're wearing now. Pull these on and you'll be fine," she said, handing her a pair of soft, black leather ballet slippers. "Bernie and I might go down to eat in the restaurant," she added as Alexa shimmied out of her stockings and pulled the slippers on.

"And leave me alone with that man?" Alexa squeaked. "What if…"

"Now you hush being silly," Janie laughed. "He's a fine, upstanding man. He's not going to ravish you…not unless you want him to," she snickered. "I can't say I'd mind it too much."

"Janie!" Alexa gasped.

"Now don't you tell Bernie I said that," Janie winked at her, giggling again. "Come on, let's not keep him waiting."

"I am *not* wearing my pajamas in front of a strange man. This will do fine!" Alexa declared archly, tugging her dress into place over her smooth, bare legs.

"Suit yourself." Janie led her back into the sitting room. "Bernie," she called out, "Are you taking me to dinner?"

"Yes, ma'am," her husband piped up, throwing an apologetic look at Alexa.

Alexa glared at the couple as Bernie hurriedly exited the suite, a bustling Janie behind him.

"We'll be back later, honey!" Janie trilled, talking to Bernie animatedly as the door closed behind her.

Alexa didn't know what to do now. With a deep breath, she turned and looked fixedly at her visitor. She wasn't sure what she was going to do with him, but whatever it was…she wouldn't back down. She stood and waited.

"So," he finally spoke.

Waves of memories washed over her at the sound of his voice. She'd been going on autopilot for days. Could this be the man that had saved her? Was it him?

"How *you* doin?" he intoned, his Joey Tribiani-voice firmly in place.

She stared at him, stunned, and then burst into laughter. He grinned, his full lips curving to reveal even, white teeth. Still giggling, she sank to the couch, holding her sides.

"I was all worried and afraid, and you, you…" she dissolved again into gales of laughter. "I can't believe you!"

"I can't be serious every minute, hmmm?" he moved closer to her. "You look a bit more comfortable, *cara*," Andrei purred in his mildly accented voice.

The sound of it stroked across her senses like a cat's tongue, causing Alexa to shiver. She wandered over to a carved sideboard that housed several bottles of liquor and alcohol.

"I, um, I should offer you something to drink, shouldn't I?" she asked uneasily, noticing that he'd removed his suit jacket. "I'm afraid I don't entertain much, Mr. Di Claudio," she offered with a shrug. He might as well know that she was a social cripple and liked it that way.

"Come, Alexa," he murmured into her ear as his hands stroked down each arm. She started and his light chuckle sent the blood pounding through her veins as heat pooled in the pit of her stomach. "Naldo will bring us a light snack and a bottle of wine. Come sit with me."

He wrapped an arm around her shoulders and steered her toward a small, elegant sofa just as Naldo entered with a tray holding an assortment of breads and cheeses, and a bottle of red wine with two glasses.

"Thank you, Naldo, that will be all for tonight," Andrei instructed him. With a nod of acquiescence, the other man left the suite.

Alexa went immediately on her guard when Andrei dismissed his man for the rest of the night. "I—I don't know you and..." she began to protest, attempting to move away from him.

"Shh, *cara*," he soothed her, rubbing the back of her neck gently.

His touch sent her nerves rocketing out of control. Withdrawing his hand, he filled two glasses with wine and handed one to her. He leaned back into the corner of the couch and sipped from his glass, arching a brow and inclining his head toward the plate of breads and cheeses.

She looked at him with every intention of telling him to leave her alone, but somehow, she couldn't. His firm jaw, his riveting black eyes framed by long thick lashes, strong, sculpted cheekbones and full black brows, she couldn't tear her eyes from his face. Her eyes traveled to his full mouth and she found herself staring.

The moment was broken when he leaned forward, lifting a cube of cheese in his tapered fingers, and nudging her lips with it. She opened her mouth only wide enough to accommodate the small morsel and he pushed it onto her teeth, caressing her lower lip with his finger. When she'd chewed it for a moment, he handed her a glass of the wine. She sipped it, watching him intently. With a half-smile, he placed an assortment of cheese cubes and bread cubes on a little plate and handed it to her. She blushed and took it, curling her legs under her, and sitting back.

"I don't mix with other people much, Mr. Di Claudio," she confessed, nibbling at the cheese and sipping the wine.

"You will call me Andrei, Alexa," he insisted firmly, his tone brooking no argument. "I am pleased that you don't go out with many men," he answered her earlier statement.

"I don't go out with anyone, Andrei," she looked at him, arching a brow and stressing her use of his first name. "Now that I think about it," she narrowed her eyes at him. "That suits me fine."

"It suits me fine as well, bellissima," he agreed smugly. "You shall go out with me and I am not simply anyone. I am Andrei Di Claudio."

"Well *bully* for you!" Alexa snapped sharply, placing the plate of half-eaten cheese and bread on the table.

She could hardly believe his arrogance. She didn't really want the cheese anyway. She was hungry, yes. She was really hungry, and thirsty, too. She'd tried to eat and drink time and again. Nothing was right, nothing appealed. Everything just made her sick.

* * * *

Andrei hid a smile at Alexa's ferocity. She tried so hard to be tough and yet there she was, so very vulnerable. He watched her stalk across the room, a frown marring her beautiful features.

He reached out for her mind and felt the poison, the evil hiss of the insidious Balfent crawling through her thoughts. He could see that it disturbed her. It disturbed him as well.

"*Cara*," he murmured, rising and slowly moving behind her, reluctant to frighten her. Resting both hands on her hips, he pulled her back against him. "Lean on me, *cara*, it won't be as bad when we are together."

He heard her swallow and felt her stir restlessly, but she didn't pull away. "I don't know what you mean," she evaded.

"Yes, you do," he countered. "You hear him, don't you?"

"Uh," she made a small sound that could have been a gasp. "No—I...."

"Shh, don't mar your lovely mouth by uttering a lie to me, Alexa," he stopped her, his arms sliding to cross over her stomach. "I know about it—he made me as well."

"No," she denied, her voice a whisper, a cry.

"Yes, *mia* Alexa," he countered. "He made me as I am and you are halfway changed. You must know, you must have guessed," he prodded gently, firmly.

"I don't want to be whatever this is. I'm only ill. It's an infection, from the attack," she denied to him.

"Well, *bella*, that is indeed a clever way to call it. An infection."

"What do you mean?" Her voice was high. "Do you...you can't mean that you really believe in vampires?"

"How can I not?" he murmured, turning her to face him.

He took her forefinger between his index finger and thumb, bringing the tip to his sharp incisor. Her brow furrowed as she touched the pointed tooth. Still staring into her eyes, he brought her finger to her own mouth.

"No!" she cried in denial, avoiding the proof. "No, no, no," she moaned, shaking her head and trying to twist away from him.

"Hush, Alexa, stop," he ordered softly, catching her as she crumpled against him. Carefully he lifted her and carried her to the couch. Stroking her hair, he soothed and calmed her, letting her cry.

"It's not fair!" she wailed. "I don't want this! This is wrong! It's—it's obscene!"

"Yes, *cara*, it is," he agreed as she began to subside. "I had no more choice than you. If I could have prevented it for you, I would have, I swear it."

She sighed heavily on a choked sob, nestling against him. He was certain she didn't even realize that she was cuddling closer. He knew she wasn't outgoing. She'd made that perfectly clear.

"So what happens now? Am I a vampire? A monster like him?" her eyes flew to his face. "Oh. I didn't mean...." she trailed off, her cheeks flooded with pink.

"He is a monster unlike any other," Andrei told her seriously. "You and I will be monsters of a different sort." He leaned down and kissed her nose. "You currently find yourself in a limbo state. You are not yet a vampire but not ...normal anymore."

"Oh..." she seemed to be considering this. "Well...do I just live this way? I mean...I don't feel good very much but...well I haven't changed into a bat. And...um..."

Andrei threw back his head and laughed out loud. Tightening his arms around her, he shook his head from side to side. "*Cara mia*! A bat? You are so precious. No! You will certainly not become a disease carrying rodent!"

"It's not funny," she growled at him. "I can't eat, I can't drink, and I'm tired all the time! I don't...this is...." She burst into tears again.

Andrei felt bad. Worse than bad. Here he was laughing at her and she was going through the worst thing he could think of.

"No, Alexa, you're right, it is anything but funny. You are in a limbo state but you've taken his blood into you. He can command you with ease. In addition, you desperately need nourishment. You will have to drink from me."

"Now, wait a minute." She looked at him suspiciously, eyes narrowed. "If I drink your blood—ick by the way—won't I become your..." She rolled her eyes. "Slave!" she spat. "That's just ridiculous!"

Andrei smiled, pulling her across his lap. "You'd rather be my minion?" he chuckled, his arched brow at odds with his amused face. "*Cara*," he said. "Suppose I tell you what will happen next? That will help, I think."

She sniffed deeply and nodded.

"The way you are now, you are in between. You have supped from Balfent. He is an ancient and evil beast." She nodded, her eyes wide. "You are subject to him since he has had your blood and began to change you with his own."

She tilted her head and he knew that she didn't really understand what he meant.

"You see, by drinking the blood—by exchanging blood with a vampire, an ancient such as Balfent, you become one, but are his subject—his servant. There are ways to change that, to stop it, but as it is now, you are his."

"I—I don't want to be his. What can I do about that?" she asked, her voice shaking.

"Well, *mia* Alexa, there are few things. I and my cousins were changed by him at a time when we were injured. He turned us and made us his slaves. But we were able to break free."

"How? How did you? How will I?"

"We will first talk about how to lessen his influence on you. So far, he hasn't tested you, though I know he will. When I left you that night, I drank your essence, but only enough to find you again."

"What can we—I still don't really understand."

"He holds your blood in his body, the same as I do. Now we can always find you. We have part of you with us. The difference is that you have part of him within you, his blood. You are, quite literally, joined with his essence. You are made up of part of him."

"Ohhh…hmmm," she was clearly giving this matter serious consideration. "Then, for instance, if I drank Janie's blood, I'd be joined with her essence?"

He smiled. "Yes, except that being joined with Janie would only meet your nutritional needs. Drinking my blood will make you stronger and help combat the hold that Balfent has over you."

She looked at him for a minute. "But, won't I be under your…um, thrall?"

He shrugged. "Yes, you will. As long as you share my blood and I yours, you will be under my—influence," he grinned.

She rolled her eyes at him. "To-māto, To-măto," she said dryly.

He considered telling her of the other possibility. He considered it seriously. She could avoid being under anyone's "thrall" as she'd put it. But only if she decided to join her life to his forever as his mate. She would have to make love with him while they both drank, one from the other. He knew it was too soon for her to seriously consider that.

For now, this was the only way he could protect her. "You're aware that the idea of drinking blood grosses me out?" she leaned back on his lap and looked up at him.

"I had gathered that, yes." He tried not to smile. Life with her would be a lot of fun, he suspected. He truly hoped she eventually agreed to mate with him for all time. For the present, he just needed her to drink.

"So, what do I have to do? I mean, do I just lean over and bite you, or what?" She looked at his neck dubiously. "Well, at least you're clean. That other guy..." she let her sentence trail off as she shuddered.

"Yes," he controlled his grin this time, "I am careful to bathe regularly. Now," he shifted her against him so that her mouth was even with his Adam's apple. "All you will do is lean close to me. Put your face against my neck. Nature will take its course."

He abstractly considered the irony of telling her to let nature direct her in such an unnatural cause, but it was true. The smell of his blood, the sound of it pounding through his arteries, she would know exactly what to do.

Nervously, she did lean in, unconsciously nuzzling his neck with first her nose and then her lips. Her satin tongue darted nervously to his throat and traced the heavy vein leading to his heart.

Andrei swallowed a groan but couldn't control the hardening of his body. When her tiny, brand new fangs pierced his jugular, he moaned his arousal. He'd never felt anything like this before, he thought, as his hands dove into her thick, wavy hair. He could feel her sucking on his skin, every nerve, every pore alive with sensation as heat, want, need, throbbed through him. His sex felt heavy and sullen between his legs, his stomach tight with desire.

It took every iota of self-control he could muster to remain still and let her drink as she needed.

* * * *

At first Alexa couldn't believe that she was truly going to bite a man in the neck and suck his blood. She decided to at least follow his direction and put her face to his throat.

Andrei Di Claudio was a very attractive man. He smelled clean, manly, sexy. When she moved her face against his throat, she found herself overwhelmed with an urgency she couldn't name.

She could hear the sound of his blood rushing in his vein. She could smell the rich aroma of the life-giving liquid. It smelled like the richest fruit. She wanted it more than anything she'd ever wanted. She *had* to have it, to taste it. Her tongue darted out and traced the heavy artery. She tasted the salt-musk tang of him, and through his skin, she could taste just the hint of his blood.

She opened her mouth and was lost. Her fangs buried in his neck and the rich flavor of his life force flowing, bursting into her mouth. She groaned with her whole body, the feeling was more than satisfying a hunger. It was sexual. This was the most moving and intimate thing she'd ever done and she was powerless over the primal need welling up within her. She heard herself moan as she slid her splayed fingers into his long, dark satin hair.

His arms tightened around her as she cupped his head and slowed her sucking so that she was mouthing the soft velvet skin of his neck, milking the blood into her fangs.

She felt him harden against her bottom and knew he was as aroused as she was. On one level, she was frightened by what was happening. On another, it was the most intense experience of her life.

"*This is too much,*" she thought, trying to pull away but unable to.

"*Drink, Alexa, I'll stop you when it's time.*" She heard his voice in her mind clearly, as if he was speaking aloud to her and it scared her. "*You've heard the evil one already. This isn't new to you,*" he reminded her. "W*ouldn't you rather hear me than him?*"

"*It's just... overwhelming. It's overwhelming,*" she repeated mentally. "*Everything is.*" Still suckling at the small punctures in his neck, she couldn't deny it to herself, to him.

Her tongue teased at his flesh as her lips caressed him. "This joining is almost more than any other, *cara mia,*" he said aloud. "Of course it is overwhelming. You are taking my very essence into you to keep you alive. Before we part this evening, I will take some more of yours, to keep you strong within me."

She felt as if she were falling into him. With the other, Balfent, she'd felt owned, subjected. With Andrei, she was where she wanted to be. She reveled in the feelings pouring over her.

"Enough," he ordered her. "Lick the wounds closed. Your saliva has a healing agent in it and it will heal and hide the bite."

Reluctantly, she complied. Pulling back, her tongue rasped gently over the small punctures and closed them.

"And now, I'm you're slave, right?" she asked, though she didn't really feel like a slave. "Will I turn into a zombie or something?"

"No, silly woman, nothing like that," he laughed, his chuckle rich and deep. "It is that you are more likely to listen more to me than him...he will tell you to do things, order you. With me near you, you are more likely to pay attention to me than him. At least you will be divided even if you don't have complete power over your own will."

"I still don't get it," she almost whined. She really didn't.

"Well, you needed to be fed and if we're lucky you will not need more than that. Hopefully, Balfent will not bother you and you will never know the difference. I could tell you to do things and you would. But we won't do that today."

"Um, you think he will come, don't you? You don't think he's finished with me, do you?" A shiver ran over her body chasing goose bumps up her spine.

"It's not like him to just walk away. He has never walked away yet. He is still after my cousins and me, even now," he confirmed her fears.

"Nothing like trying to reassure me, is there?" Alexa gave him a crooked smile. She wasn't sure what to think. Here she was cuddled in this handsome man's lap. She'd just been drinking his blood. She was more turned on than she'd ever been in her life and he could order her to have sex with him. Somehow, she knew he wouldn't.

"You probably don't recall what happened the other night very clearly, do you? Andrei asked her.

"No, not really. Only that it was just horrible when he put his hands on me. That part, I remember very well."

"Lean back," he instructed. "I'm glad you don't remember," he murmured, his hand sweeping the length of hair off her neck and shoulders. "I will take a taste of your essence, your blood."

"Wait!" she stopped him. "What happens though? Am I a vampire? Will I become one?"

"Yes, *cara*, you are turning into a vampire. There are ways, other ways, but for now, you should understand that you are a vampire."

"That just sounds so—melodramatic." She shook her head, in confusion, in denial, maybe both.

Andrei lifted a dark brow and looked steadily at her. "You prefer being called one of the Plasma-challenged, perhaps? Does that suit your sensitivities better?"

She slapped at him. "Very funny!" she groaned. "But I can't go out in the sun and things like that, right?"

"You are what is known as a young vampire so, no, you cannot be in direct sunlight. You will tire during the full heat of the day but as the sun fades, you will find you have more energy. In time, it won't be such a challenge, although you will never frolic in the sunshine again."

She considered that a moment. "I never frolicked a lot to begin with," she shrugged. "What about sleeping?" she asked, both curious and worried.

"Sleeping? You will close your eyes and…"

"No, not that! I mean…coffins?"

He threw back his head and laughed out loud again. She couldn't help but smile. He had a wonderful, deep laugh. "Um, no, *piccola*, no coffins…unless, of course, you prefer it?" He arched a sable colored brow at her.

"No," she mumbled, sure her face was a flaming red now.

He sobered somewhat and began to explain. "You will, however, appear dead to anyone who comes upon you. It might be best to lock your door while you sleep or perhaps…"

"Perhaps?" she arched her own sculpted brow at him. "You had something to add?" she asked archly.

He looked at her long and steady, and she looked back, trying not to drop her gaze. Once again, she was struck by how very attractive he was, but not in a false way. His looks were intense and real. He didn't need to bother with subterfuge—unless one counted the fact that he was a vampire masquerading as a…. Her thoughts stuttered to a stop. How old was he?

"Perhaps you should sleep with me," he answered and she stared at him blankly. Her mind had moved on and she was shocked back to the conversation. "Alexa?" he asked after a moment.

"Um…I should sleep with you?" she squeaked. Yes she was surprised, but to be honest, that idea had more than a little appeal.

When she shifted against him, Andrei groaned. "Woman…" he growled.

She smiled seductively at him, leaning back on his arm. He nuzzled her neck and breathed in her tempting scent. His lips trailed up the delicate length, caressing, tasting. He could feel her hunger for him. It was feeding on his for her. He wanted her. He hungered for her body as much as he hungered for her blood, but he would wait.

With no further ado, he sunk his sharp fangs into the blood vessel, sustaining himself on the warm essence of her. He would swear that her blood was as rich and sweet as any wine, though he knew, academically, that all blood tasted the same.

She stretched back just enough to make more room for his head, her fingers sliding into his hair. Her desire for him heated her and scorched him. Quickly closing the tiny wounds, Andrei lifted her.

"Where are we going?" Her voice was small and confused.

"To bed, Alexa, time to sleep," he murmured, carrying her toward the door to the suite.

"I don't want to sleep," she complained, her voice a compelling and silky purr. "I want you, I want to make love," she emphasized her desire by leaning in to lick his ear. "I love your hair," she whispered, rubbing her cheek against the soft, satin black strands.

He knew that she was nearly drunk on the sensuality of their blood sharing. His own thoughts of lying with her and loving her slowly and languorously would be as clear to her as if they were her own. Add to that she did want him, was genuinely attracted to him. It was a recipe for—sex, certainly, if nothing else.

"I love your hair, too," he said and smiled, kissing the crown of her head as they entered Andrei's suite. "Naldo?" he called softly.

The other man materialized from another room, seeming unsurprised to see them. Andrei knew that he was quite surprised, but would be too professional to indicate that in any way.

"Yes, Senior Di Claudio?" Naldo asked evenly.

"Please inform Alexa's associates that she is well and with me," Andrei instructed his servant. He had no desire to mar Alexa's reputation with her employees but it couldn't be helped. Anyway, he had the clear impression that at least Janie would be pleased with this turn of events.

He hoped that Alexa would voluntarily join with him in time. For now, they certainly would seem to be having an affair together. It would continue in this fashion as long as Balfent was a threat. Things were complicated enough and he knew he was asking for trouble. Still he believed she'd be safer sleeping with him than she would on her own. The evil that had stalked him and his cousins for two centuries would now be hunting her. She would be easy game.

He carefully laid her down on his bed, one arm on either side of her head. "Andrei?" she whispered. "Are you...?"

"Shh," he cut her off, laying a finger across her lips. "We are sleeping," he stated firmly.

Her lush mouth turned down in a pout. "I want to do more than sleep," she complained.

"So do I, cara," he murmured, "And that's probably why you do. But tonight, we are sleeping." He looked long and deeply into her eyes.

It didn't take much for him to mesmerize her. She was primed for his suggestion and he concentrated on making her sleep. Her eyes drooped closed and she slipped into a heavy, trancelike slumber.

With a deep sigh, he straightened, and then groaned aloud, cursing himself for his shortsightedness. He had wanted to make her sleep and control her amorous advances. He had, only now she was in his bed but fully dressed. She hadn't even washed her face.

He didn't know all the trouble women went through with makeup and things. He was sure, though, that she would have at least cleaned it off. He hoped she'd done a bit of that while arguing with Janie in her bedroom. That really wasn't his main concern. After all, vampires were exempt from little irritants like acne and skin blemishes. No, the problem was that she would need to be stripped of that heavy, clingy, one piece dress. He certainly wouldn't call upon Naldo to do it nor would he call her helper, Janie. That left only him to undress her and cover her again.

He found himself fighting his own desires as he tugged and pulled, finally freeing her of the hated garment. He stood for a moment, just staring at her relaxed face, young and beautiful, a wavy fan of satin hair framing her upper body.

Alexa was a shapely young woman in her prime, with full and generous breasts highlighted by a delicate, antique lace bra that revealed more than it concealed. He followed the beautiful line of her body down to a narrow waist and flared, rounded hips.

A thin band of elastic supported a strip of satin and lace that he suspected was a thong. He'd seen many of them in recent years. To see her beautiful body accented by such frippery, he just wasn't ready.

With a flick of his wrist, he covered her with a blanket, quickly stripped down to his boxer shorts, and joined her. While there were a few hours yet until the dawn, Andrei found he had no desire to be anywhere else. All his appetites were in this bed.

Chapter Five

Alexa awoke in a strange room and in a strange bed, awareness of her surroundings slowly creeping in on her. There was…a man! She was in bed with a man!

It was Andrei Di Claudio, the man who'd saved her from that squirmy vampire. She combed the hair out of her face with her fingers and looked down at her companion, noting that she still wore her bra and panties.

The sound of the ancient vampire's whispery hiss echoed in her head. "Come to me, dear one, come to me," he chanted over and over. She shuddered. But Andrei had chased him away from her, had chased that insidious voice away. Even last night, when she thought she'd go crazy from the whispering, he'd come and made it go away. She rose to her knees and turned to him.

Looking at his handsome, boyish face, full lips, strong cheekbones and chin, she felt a hunger stir in the pit of her belly. Gingerly, she reached out and touched his face. It was cool but warmed to her fingers as she stroked his cheek. Had he been dead, as the old stories told? Would she be that way, too? Had she been?

The whisper of the old vampire, Balfent, played through her thoughts and she struggled against its compelling pull on her. It frightened her, how strong the urge was to go to him, to answer his call. Stronger still was the urge, the need to stay with the man next to her. And he wanted her. Yes, Andrei was asleep, but somehow, she knew he desired her.

Her fingertips trailed down his jaw to his neck and she thought of what they'd done the night before. Her heart thumped and her pussy tightened. She could feel her breathing speed up as she leaned down to him.

He didn't stir but she could hear his heart beating. She could smell the blood scent mixed with his own unique, masculine smell. It was a heady mix and she touched her pointed incisors with her tongue, excited to feel them lengthen. The night before, he'd bitten her—she'd bitten him. They'd had each other's blood. It had been the most erotic experience of her life.

A hunger like none she'd ever felt before pushed her as she moved over him, straddling his thighs with her own. His healthy, full erection poked through the opening in his boxers and she scooted back to inspect it. It was large, thick, with a wrinkle of gathered foreskin, pushed aside by the full width of his engorged head. The mushroom shaped bulb was curved, smooth and shiny.

"Alexa? What…" Andrei was waking up.

She smiled at his sleepy, confused face and leaned down to the flared, purple head of his cock.

The tangy, musky scent of his arousal teased her. As she watched, a small, clear drop of fluid oozed from the slit. With a half-smile, she leaned down, touching the tip of her tongue to it and scooping it out.

"Ahhhh," he moaned, flexing his hips reflexively, unconsciously asking for more.

With a sly half-smile, Alexa raked her fingernails through the sable curls at the base of his throbbing erection. "I should do that again," she murmured when he groaned.

"Ohhh, Alexaaaa," he hissed when she swirled her tongue around the rounded top as if it were an ice cream cone.

As his hips pumped up, she gripped the velvet steel rod, gathering silk and curly hair as she did. She let his cock slide into her mouth and all the way to the back of her throat, working her tongue back and forth over the thick vein underneath. Sucking lightly, she moved back up the shaft, working it with her hand as she let it slide to her lips and then sucked it back in.

Andrei gripped the sheets and seemed to be struggling not to thrust into her mouth. Grinning, she let his leaking erection slip out of her mouth, pushing her lacy thong off her hips at the same time.

"Stop this, Alexa," Andrei groaned, scooting back toward the head of the bed.

Flicking the closure on her bra, Alexa grinned at him. "You don't want me to stop, Andrei. I can read your thoughts, too. That's how I knew what to do." She shrugged out of the satin confection and threw her shoulders back in a wanton stretch.

"The time is not right for us, Alexa," he tried again, looking slightly desperate as she dropped back onto her hands and knees and crawled toward him.

"Oh, but I think it is," she argued, rocking forward to take a sensitive, pebbled nipple between her teeth. Tracing the pulsing vein up from the flat, bumpy nub, she lapped at it, wanting nothing more than to sink her teeth into it while he sunk deep into her. Maybe he would drink from her at the same time. She felt her own excitement weep from between her legs.

"Please, Andrei," she whispered, up and down his hairless chest with her tongue, following the artery.

"You torture me," he groaned. "I saved you to torture me!"

"Make love to me or I'll go find someone else—Naldo maybe," she bluffed, knowing it was an empty threat, she was sure he did, too. Regardless, the same deception had worked in every romance novel she'd ever read, she was sure it would work now.

With a muted roar, Andrei didn't disappoint, flipping her onto her back and covering her body with his own. "Never, never speak such foolishness to me again," he growled, nipping at her throat, sucking a little blood and licking the punctures closed.

Kissing and nipping his way down to one peaked breast, he took the whole thing into his mouth sucking hard and then released it. She moaned as he sank his fangs into the artery there. He sipped from it, closed the wounds, and moved to its twin, nipping and drinking from her once again.

"Andrei, please," she whimpered when he lifted his head. She barely recognized her own voice, moaning and begging for something, anything that he would give her.

"You are not pleased, *Cara mia*?" he purred, nipping at the tender flesh of her ribs with his front teeth. "I will try harder to please you, then."

He buried his hot tongue in the hollow of her belly button and she arched her back, groaning and tossing her head. Andrei slid her thighs onto his heavy biceps spreading her open to him. Shocked and unsure, she looked into his steady black eyes, his gaze riveted intently on hers.

She sucked in a deep breath and thought, just for a second, that she saw something move behind his eyes. With a low growl, he plunged his tongue into her soaking heat and scraped her clit with his teeth, burying his fangs in the rich veins on either side of her inner labia.

A wave of the most intense pleasure and pain she'd ever felt swept her and she screamed, rocking her hips up and pressing harder into his mouth. The world dimmed around her for a moment and she thought she would pass out.

"Oh my god, oh my god, oh my god," she chanted, unable to say anything else.

Andrei surged up her body and slid into her, spreading her wide and filling her completely. As if from a distance, she felt the thin membrane of her hymen give way. He obviously felt it too. She was sure his growl this time was one of satisfaction.

"Feed from me, *cara*," he told her as, with one hand, he pulled her leg over his hip.

He was leaning mostly on his left elbow, his palm cupping her head. She lifted her face to his chest, the sharp points of her small fangs scraping her tongue.

Finding the artery, she wasted no time. Hunger spiraled through her, driving her. She wanted him to fill her body while his essence filled her mouth. She sunk her new fangs into him as he plunged once again, deep inside.

All the feelings, all the emotions, wrapped around her like a cloud of fine silk, cocooning her in this new and sensual world of touch and taste. She felt the smooth slide of Andrei's cock, in and out, and his hot blood flowing into her. Up and up, higher and higher the cyclone of sensations climbed, the body rocking explosion took her utterly by surprise, carrying her completely away.

Chapter Six

Would you do anything for me?
Something, Anything
Just for me,
Anything, Anything at all
Do you feel anything for me?

Andrei stood in his box, his eyes and ears riveted on Alexa as she sang, though his mind replayed the events of their lovemaking over and over. He'd had sex, and made love, millions of times in his long life.

This time, today, waking up to Alexa with her delicate fingers skimming over his skin, her soft, warm breath caressing over his throbbing cock...this time was the first time he'd been moved, honestly moved, while making love. This time he knew it was the real thing.

Listening to her singing her signature song, Andrei nodded to himself. He would do anything for her. *Anything*. There was no doubt, no question.

As he considered the lengths that he might have to go to for her, Andrei heard the hiss, the malevolent whisper crawl through his mind.

"Anything, boy? Anything? Yessss. You may be willing to do anything for her. Fool. There isn't anything you can do to keep me from having her."

Andrei started, hearing Alexa's voice catch in mid-note. She'd heard the same thing he had. The foul presence of the ancient, evil creature slid from his psyche and Andrei closed his eyes, concentrating on the song Alexa was singing and remembering the feel of his hard shaft, sliding in and out of her clinging heat. In and out, the ancient rhythm of two bodies in perfect harmony, her tight channel stroking his aching cock. Beautiful. Perfect. He felt her relax into him, her thoughts accepting him, her voice smoothing into a sensual satin melody.

I would do anything
I would give anything
I guess there isn't anything
To bring you to me...

She closed her eyes, moving into the microphone, her mind playing back to him the soul deep comfort of belonging he'd experienced as her leg had slid around his hip, her arms around his neck as she drank from him. Yes, she was home for him. She was all he needed in his extensive life.

He saw her lips curl in a satisfied smile as she sang the closing bars of the song. She was beginning to know his thoughts as intimately as he did himself. She wasn't completely vampire yet, but she wasn't far off. If she chose not to live an eternity with him, he would share her life with her and end his when the time came. It was difficult to kill a vampire, but not impossible. Nothing was impossible. Freeing her from Balfent wouldn't be impossible, just difficult.

* * * *

Alexa bowed and thanked her audience, brushing the clinging hair from her sweat soaked forehead and cheek. "You've been wonderful to me." She smiled and added, "It's been an honor to sing to you tonight."

She smiled and glanced up toward the box where she knew Andrei watched her. She was a little embarrassed still. She'd wantonly attacked him this afternoon. She'd initiated sex—well, that was an understatement.

His desire had flowed through her and she'd wanted it. She'd wanted his desire and she'd wanted their lovemaking. Maybe she could blame it on this whole vampire thing, but that would really be lying to herself—not something she would allow herself to do.

She wished she had more information about what was happening to her. She could feel her body changing. She seldom even felt hungry or thirsty. Certainly, her appetites were not the same as they'd been in the past, anyway. Compared to how she'd felt the night before, she was a new woman.

"*Yes, precious, a new woman. Myyy woman. Just as your lover is my boy. Mineeee*," she heard the cruel whine of the high-pitched whisper that grated across her mind like fingernails on a chalkboard.

"Alexa, that was wonderful, honey," Janie chattered. "You have been so much better today than all last week." Her voice dropped an octave. "I told you he was hot, didn't I? Alexa? Honey? Are you all right?" Alexa was trembling, unable to hide it from the older woman.

Where was Andrei? Was that monster nearby? Would he get her? Would he get Andrei? What if he did? What could she do?

"Alexa," there was Andrei, finally. His arm slid across her back and around her shoulders. He pulled her against his chest, murmuring, "Calm, *cara*, calm yourself. You are safe. Water, please, Janie?" He smiled at Janie who scampered off ahead, only too happy to have a purpose, a way to help.

"Andrei," she choked, "he was there, right in my head. Right there, again, and he said, he said…" she shivered, fighting back tears and fear.

"Shh, *cara mia*," he kissed her temple. "I heard him, too. That's his weakness. I hear what he says when you do. He won't win you."

"But you, Andrei, he said you were his, that you belonged to him."

"And once I was, Alexa." He guided her toward the long hallway leading to her dressing room. Janie could be seen rushing toward them with a bottle of water clutched in her wide hand. "We will be there in moments, Janie, wait for us inside," he instructed, his voice taking on a smooth and compelling timbre.

Janie turned with a vacant smile and headed back down the hall toward the dressing room. Alexa glanced up at Andrei feeling her heart rush to double time. With just a few words in a different tone of voice, Andrei could make people do things. Had he done that to her? When?

"Hush, Alexa, stop," he halted her galloping thoughts. "You are safe and I have never manipulated you beyond a drink of water and much needed sleep. You know that."

She sighed and nodded. She did know that. Even though she read his thoughts, even been a little influenced by them, she hadn't been enthralled. She had been intrigued. She had to believe that. She knew he wouldn't want her to come to him of anything but her own free will.

In fact, he'd tried to stop her today when she'd known without a doubt that he wanted her. She'd argued, she'd manipulated, not him. She'd had sex with him entirely of her own volition and she wasn't in any way sorry.

"Nor am I, *cara*," he whispered. "Now, shall we join your friends?"

"Are you always going to do that?" she asked, trying to act a little put out.

95

Andrei wasn't fooled. "As often as you do, Alexa." He squeezed her shoulder and guided her down the hall and into her dressing room.

"Alexa, how are you, honey? You certainly look better." Janie sounded both relieved and urgent.

"I'm fine, Janie," Alexa responded, smiling fondly.

The events of the last week had taken their toll on her. Letting Andrei in had made her face more than physical feelings. She did love, she needed, just as everyone else did. The couple waiting for her now was more than employees. They were her family.

"Alexa, I will leave you with Janie and Bernie while I go and find us something to dine on, shall I?" Andrei stared at her steadily.

Alexa felt a moment of panic. He was going to leave her and that nasty vampire was around somewhere. What would she do if that horrible creature showed up? How would she fight him off?

"Isn't that sweet?" Janie asked, aiming a satisfied smirk at Alexa. "He's going to go out and get you some dinner while you rest. What a thoughtful young man, Alexa." Her arm snaked around Alexa's waist in a pleased little hug.

"If you stay inside, cara, he cannot come in. I won't be long. We must feed."

"And what will I do while you're gone? Will you just bring someone back to the room or something? How does this work?"

"Janie, I leave my darling Alexa in your more than capable hands," Andrei told her smoothly. "I trust you to make sure she rests as she should," he said, one eye lowered in a devastating wink, "Just as you always have, of course." His full lips curved in a compelling and sexy smile.

"Of course, Mr. Di Claudio, of course." Janie blushed and practically giggled.

"I will find a likely candidate or two and drink enough for both of us. When I return, you shall feed from me, hmmm?"

Alexa felt the excitement curl in the pit of her stomach. Her heart thudded in her chest, awareness centering between her legs. It was such a sensual experience, all consuming, and erotic. The very idea of it made her tingle with desire.

"Well young lady, you have *so* much to tell me! Isn't he just the most handsome thing you've ever seen?" Janie continued to chatter at her, never noticing that Alexa's mind was definitely somewhere else. "Oh, of course Bernie's the most handsome man *I've* ever seen, but you have to admit that Mr. Di Claudio is very, very…."

Alexa tuned her out as she sipped at the water. Andrei had been talking to Bernie and turned at the door, stopping to look at her.

"Stay inside the suite, cara, I shall return soon," he bade her, appearing just to leave her with an affectionate smile. And then he was gone.

* * * *

Andrei felt uneasy. He was sure that Balfant wasn't far away and he wanted nothing more than to find someone to drink from and rush back to Alexa. The problem was that he needed more than he could take from one person. He needed enough for both of them.

Although part of his mind accepted that Alexa would eventually need to take blood from someone other than him, he refused to consider it right now. The practical reason was that he needed to keep her tied to him, for her own safety. The reality was that he was jealous of the idea that her lips would touch, would taste, would caress anyone else's skin, man or woman. Hopefully he wouldn't always feel quite this possessive.

Banishing all thoughts of Alexa and other people's skin, he moved silently through the all concealing night, seeking his prey. While his body could process out most impurities such as alcohol or drugs, he preferred to sup from healthy, clean living people. His cousin, Adrien, had told him once that you could feel the high for just a moment if the "donor" was drugged enough. Andrei shuddered. He'd rather benefit from rich, fresh blood with no taint.

That in mind, he headed for the city's large park, and with it, a jogging trail. If a man or woman took the time to jog, chances were good that they cared enough for their bodies to treat them right.

As he neared the almost deserted park, Andrei heard his victims approaching from opposite directions. This couldn't have worked better if he'd choreographed it. He stepped into the jogging path just as a healthy blond woman clad in brief shorts and a sporting a bouncing ponytail passed the tree near where he stood.

Andrei reached out and grabbed her, pulling her squirming athletic body against his chest. She screamed on impact and he quickly turned her to face him. Scanning her terrified thoughts, he realized that she expected the worst from him. He plucked her name from the churning morass of panic and attempted to calm her down.

"Shh, Sheila," he murmured, looking hard into her eyes. She nodded. "Lean against that tree," he instructed as he heard the heavy tread of a large man jog up the path toward them.

Without a word, the blond woman, Sheila, turned and walked toward the tree he'd indicated. It was just beyond the circle of bright yellow created by a streetlight nearby. Standing as she was, the woman looked out of place. Her would-be rescuer pounded up the path toward her.

"Lady! Lady, are you all right?" The hulking runner rounded the curve, his heart pumping adrenaline as he rushed to rescue the fair damsel.

In the moment that he snatched the white knight in sweats off the park path, Andrei learned that this gentleman wasn't there by accident this evening. The man, Walter Showalter, had been hoping to run into the fair Sheila one way or another. He'd had a crush of sorts on the fit young woman and had planned to overtake her. Tonight, Walter had decided, would be his night. It seemed that this time, Andrei could play Cupid—with fangs instead of bow and arrow.

"Hey, buddy!" Walter protested. Standing an inch or two taller than Andrei, he thought that he could overpower him; the adrenaline coursing through his bloodstream gave him the added impetus to try. "What'd you do to her?" he growled, hooking a leg behind Andrei's, intent on overbalancing him.

Andrei stepped into the heat of Walter's body and turned, as graceful as a dancer, extending his arm and lifting the taller man by his throat. Stunned, Walter's mouth dropped open and he stared into Andrei's eyes.

His dark gaze enthralled the bigger man and Andrei smiled. "Come with me, Walter," Andrei murmured.

"Uh, sure," Walter agreed when his feet touched the ground.

"Stand against the tree, Walter," Andrei instructed, his lips curving as Walter nodded, absently rubbing his throat. He'd lifted the other man by the throat, yes, but he'd learned over the years how to hold someone without bruising. Walter would be sore for a day or two but he wouldn't bruise. He'd be fine.

Andrei turned his attention to Sheila. "Come here, Sheila, I want to tell you something," he murmured.

"Okay," Sheila mumbled, her eyes wide and unfocused.

"Closer, Sheila," Andrei smiled, "It's about Walter."

Although her expression never changed, Andrei saw the young woman smile. He bent his head as if to whisper into her ear. Instead, he tilted her head to the side and sunk his teeth deep into her jugular, the pulse constant, not racing, perfect.

He drank unceasing for some minutes before he lifted his head. Sheila wasn't a large woman and he couldn't drink too much from her.

"Go stand next to Walter, Sheila, he's going to save you," Andrei told her, giving her a little push.

"Save me?" Sheila's eyes widened in childlike curiosity and wonder. "What's he gonna save me from?" Her voice sounded young, unaffected by life's disappointments and woes.

"He will save you from awful muggers and gang members. He really likes you, Sheila. Come here Walter."

Walter stood upright from his lounging stance against the wide tree trunk. He moved toward Andrei without question, his eyes half closed and every bit as unfocused as Sheila's had been.

"Sheila likes you, too, Walter," Andrei informed him, pulling him closer and lifting the big man's arm, as if to kiss his hand. Tracing the area just above the knuckles, he sunk his teeth into the wide artery traversing the back of Walter's large hand He supped from him for several minutes before he judged he'd had as much as the other man could spare. Licking the punctures closed, Andrei raised his head.

"Come, Walter," he murmured.

Giving the tall man a little push, he guided him back to Sheila. Andrei moved over and brought the two together, wrapping Walter's arms around her.

"Sheila," he said, looking deeply into her eyes, "you were attacked by a couple of young men who wanted to rob you, perhaps worse. You didn't get a clear look at the two. Walter came upon you and saved you. You feel very safe with him. It's nice you're so attracted to him. Perhaps you have fallen for him at first sight." He shifted his gaze to Walter. "Thank heaven that you saw the young men attacking Sheila. She remained unhurt thanks to you. You must always care for her. She is a precious woman."

He stepped back away from the couple, pleased with himself. Andrei, the matchmaking vampire, he smiled to himself. Well, his cousins had long teased him for his romantic streak.

Suddenly a ripple of unease coursed through him. He'd been so focused on the two runners that he had forgotten Alexa's safety. Now, he could hear the low hum of Balfent's voice in his head. She was in danger.

Chapter Seven

Alexa rolled on the bed. She'd gone to lie down shortly after Andrei had gone. Janie and Bernie had chatted with her a little but she'd been unable to concentrate on the conversation. She was worried and uneasy. She hated to be such a big baby but she was. He wasn't there now and Alexa felt defenseless. Worse than that, he was out there—out there with that awful beast. She forced herself to calm.

She drifted in and out of a light doze comforted by the sounds of Bernie and Janie preparing for bed. Water running in another room. They must be going to bed. It was late. She heard their light conversation fade away and rolled over. There, their bedroom door closing. A scrape of a chair, or was that something else?

She sat up, shaking the sleepy feeling off when she heard it. A multi-paned door was rattling. How could that be? She was in the penthouse of a very tall hotel. There was no way someone was trying to come in from the balcony. Had Janie opened the French doors to the balcony?

Alexa's blood ran cold. Andrei had said to stay inside. She was sure that he'd meant that they should keep the doors to the outside closed as well. She was *certain* that he'd meant that.

Before she could even call out to Andrei mentally, the cold hiss of Balfent's high-pitched whisper sounded in her head. *"Come to me, dear one. Come little Alexa."*

For a moment, maybe two, Alexa struggled against the directive. *"Come, Alexa, your master calls you..."* Against her will, Alexa slid off the wide bed and stood. Some part of her consciousness knew what was happening. Some part of her understood that she was in the thrall of the ancient vampire. Powerless to resist, Alexa moved toward the door to her bedroom and out into the main room.

The French doors stood open and the light silk curtains ruffled in the night's slightly cool breeze. She made note of all these things as she moved slowly toward the doors thrown wide. Janie and Bernie were nowhere in sight.

She felt a curl of fear as she realized that the hideous demon might have hurt them somehow. Her internal struggle waged on as she moved slowly toward the gaping doors.

"Fear not, beloved, I haven't harmed your helpers. Even now, they are downstairs, eating the second meal of the night. Full but still dining as instructed."

The whispered communiqué floated through her thoughts although it didn't reassure her overmuch. She was sure that, if this creature could take over someone's life on a whim, he would have no qualms about lying to assure her smooth cooperation.

"Faster, girl, move faster, come!" Balfent's impatience was a living thing and Alexa had no choice but to move faster, though she tried so hard to fight it.

Soon she found herself standing on the cold, stone balcony, tiny points of light in the inky sky clear to her and scattered clusters below still part of the vista. Directly in front of her, she saw the creature, now looking amazingly dapper, like an old British gentleman out for a stroll.

That would have been believable, even to her, but for two things. His eyes glowed dangerous, bestial red in the dark night, and he stood on the thick railing of the balcony, his stance casual almost. The scene was beyond surreal as he balanced negligently, more than ten stories from the ground.

With unbelievable grace, he stepped lightly to the stone floor, sweeping a hand wide and scattering the tasteful deck table and chairs out of her path, clearing the way to him. The wind wasn't strong enough for such a thing; there was barely a breeze. Alexa could only imagine some psychic ability aided in his seemingly magical command.

"My newest little trinket," he murmured, *"come closer to me, come."*

Helpless, she did as commanded, stepping nearer and then reluctantly nearer still, her dress brushing against him. On the inside, she shuddered in distaste, but to anyone looking on, she would appear docile and accepting.

"Tilt your head, dearest," he ordered her almost lovingly, *"It seems you find me too easy to resist. And look, look how weak you are! I must feed you!"*

"No!!" Alexa's mind screamed. *"Andrei! Please make this stop!"*

Balfent's echoing laughter seemed to fill up every corner of her head, pushing out any of her own thoughts. As if from far away, she saw the old vampire slice his wrist with a long, sharp fingernail. He lifted the bleeding cut to her face.

Alexa worked not to part her lips, but to no avail. Balfent grabbed a handful of her long hair and pulled hard to the side. When she gasped with pain, he pressed his cut forearm to her mouth. At the same time, he buried his needle sharp incisors in her artery, drinking greedily.

Try as she might not to swallow the vile fluid, Alexa felt some of it trickle down her throat. Her struggles were as effective as the swat of a kitten's paw, desperation bled away to despair. She knew acceptance wasn't far behind.

* * * *

"*Your master calls to you...*"

Andrei heard the dreaded rasp of his maker's voice and knew it was to Alexa that the old one was calling. Driven by a fear deeper than he'd felt in a century or more, he sped toward the hotel, toward Alexa, praying as he did that he wasn't too late.

The sidewalks surrounding the hotel and concert arena were busy, glutted with fans still milling about. After one second of indecision, Andrei decided that he could propel himself upward, at a speed that would protect him from gawking bystanders.

Cursing himself for his hesitancy, Andrei made his way from balcony to balcony, fearing the worst. While usually the penthouse suite was preferable, he now had occasion to wish that he'd chosen convenience over luxury.

"*Andrei! Please make this stop!*" he heard and his blood ran cold.

Finally, he reached the balcony where Alexa stood, seemingly docile, in the loathsome embrace of the demon, Balfent. Not bothering to consider the scene either way, Andrei grabbed the old vampire by the back of the neck, ripping him away from Alexa like a parasitic insect.

Balfent's objection was the growling hiss of an angry cat as blood flowed from his wrist. Without a second thought, Andrei flung him backward to sprawl with an ungainly clatter in a heap on top of the displaced balcony furniture.

He wanted to care for Alexa but knew that he couldn't turn his back on Balfent. Blood was pouring from a second wound, his neck had been sliced by the shattered glass tabletop when he'd landed.

Not allowing a moment for the aged fiend to regroup, Andrei pounced on him. There was no doubt that he couldn't kill him by himself, each of the cousins had tried. In defiance of this knowledge, he grabbed him by the neck, determined to do damage at the very least. The ancient vampire hissed, eyes glowing a hellfire red, he clawed at Andrei's face, dragging ribbons of blood from behind his ear and down his throat.

"You won't bessst me, boy!" The cry echoed in the open space and through the night—possibly spoken, possibly thought, but certainly screamed.

Giving no thought to a verbal response, Andrei threw Balfent against the cement balcony rail where he bounced forward against the jutting alcove of the French doors. The backward momentum of his impact was such that he was propelled back again, his calves hitting the railing hard. With a powerful arc of his arm, Andrei swept the hated creature the rest of the way over and off, taking a moment to watch him swim threw the air, flailing toward the pavement hundreds of feet to go.

He knew the old one wouldn't be killed. Even so, he counted on the injuries the old vampire had suffered to buy himself and Alexa a little time to recover and become stronger. He hated that the beast had taken her blood and feared what the reviled creature's blood had done to her.

Alexa was kneeling to the right of the balcony doors on her hands and knees, retching and heaving as she tried to purge herself of the demon blood she'd taken in.

"How are you, Alexa?" he murmured, leaning down to help her to her feet.

"Is he—is he dead?" she choked, clinging to him weakly.

She was shaking with blood loss and possibly shock. Andrei had to remind himself that she was still very much a fledgling and very weak. Turning her, he wrapped an arm around her, leading her through her suite and into his own.

"Naldo!" he called as he entered the suite. He should have ordered Naldo to stay with her he chided himself. "Naldo!" he bellowed again, nearly at his bedroom door.

"Right here, *Senior* Di Claudio," Naldo said from beside him. The poor man had probably spoken already but Andrei was too agitated. He knew he needed to calm down.

His arm still around Alexa, Andrei turned to his servant. "There is a—mess on the balcony to the *Signorina's* suite. Please see to it."

"Right away," Naldo agreed with a deferential nod.

Andrei knew that he could trust the other man and that all would be handled with his usual aplomb. He could cease worrying about the mess but... Janie and Bernie!

"Naldo!" he shouted before the other man could exit the suite.

"*Si, Senior?*" Naldo halted and turned.

"Please locate Janie and Bernie," Andrei instructed him. Naldo nodded. "Only alert me if there is cause for concern." With another sharp nod, Naldo left the room.

* * * *

Alexa leaned heavily against Andrei as he turned again and led her into the master bedroom and the master bath. She didn't say a thing and he stripped her clothes off, reaching around her to turn on the shower.

When he would have put her into the shower alone, she grabbed at him, clinging and afraid. She didn't want him to leave. She knew it was irrational but she was afraid that the old vampire would come back. Or worse than that, he would call her to him again and she would come.

"Please, please don't leave me, Andrei," she begged. "Please stay and don't leave me alone."

"Shhh, Alexa, I'll stay," he assured her, pealing his clothes off, tossing them aside.

His muscular body emerged slowly. She didn't want to move beyond arm's reach of him and it inhibited his progress somewhat. Finally, he guided her under the warm spray of the dual showers, shaking his head to clear the water from his eyes.

She felt cold all over, shivering and shaking. She pressed herself to him, holding on tight. "I was sleeping," she mumbled as she began to explain. "I heard something." Her story was cut short by the chattering of her teeth and she began to sob.

Andrei wrapped his arms around her. "Shh, don't worry, I'm here now. I will keep you safe." He poured shampoo onto her head liberally, lathering her hair and her body, soaping her all over. "We will rid your body of the stench of him. And then you must feed from me, drink, and clear the taste of him away."

She turned left and right allowing him to manipulate her, just glad that he was with her. She knew, just knew that no harm would come to her when he was with her.

104

Andrei pulled her back under the water again, tipping her chin so that he could look into her face. "You are weak, Alexa. You must drink now, come."

He bent toward her and she stood on her toes, lifting her arms around his neck. "Make love to me, Andrei, and I will," she wheedled.

"You're weak right now. We can…"

"No!" she shouted, raising her leg and pushing off the slick floor with her other. With both legs wrapped around his waist she demanded, "Make love to me, fuck me, right now. Or I won't drink ever again!"

She knew it was childish. It didn't matter right then, she wanted it. She had to have him inside her, to prove that she was real, alive, and there with him. She'd do anything to feel, to verify life, to prove she was real and safe from that awful predator.

With a low growl, Andrei walked her back, up against the tiled wall of the shower stall. Sliding both hands under her thighs, he lifted her and set her upon his jutting erection.

Slowly, so slowly the rigid length of it penetrated her, filling her as gravity pulled her down onto his erection. "Fuck me, Andrei," she whispered, "Please? Hard, fast, I need you."

"Drink," he rasped.

She pressed her face to his clavicle, licking the smooth tanned skin stretching across the prominent bone and following it up to the bend of his throat. Without pause, she opened her mouth and sank her pointed fangs into the thick vein.

He rumbled low in his throat and lifted her higher on the wall, pulling his hips back and plunging into her, rhythmically, steadily. All the way out until just the head of his cock rested inside her and all the way in, not too fast, not too slow, he continued to pump.

Alexa lifted her head and closed the wounds. "Harder", she demanded.

Andrei growled an objection, stopping. "Drink!" he ordered.

"No," she narrowed her eyes, glaring at him. "Harder!"

He braced both arms on the wall on either side of her head. "Hold on," he growled at her, pressing her bodily against the wall.

She nodded, clutching tightly at him. Suddenly he began to piston into her jackhammer fast and hard, his pelvis rubbing her clit with every stroke.

"Yes, yes, oh my god, yes," she sobbed, as his thick, silky pubic hair rasped against her sensitive lips and his thick shaft continued to plunge.

Suddenly he stopped, pulled back, one arm now holding her fast against him, the other braced against the slick tile wall, Andrei thrust upward, hard. His release roared out of him filling her with heat. She felt like her soul had exploded super nova around them as she collapsed, limp in his arms.

Still holding her, still embedded deeply in her, he turned around in the shower, rinsing them both. With a concentrated glare, the faucet turned off, the water trickling to a drip. Kicking open the stall door, he didn't pull out, just snatched a towel as he carried her to the large bed, laying her down and following her as he did.

"Drink," he murmured, and she traced the large vein above his heart with her tongue, eyes closed. She buried her incisors in his pounding artery and began to drink.

The feelings that joining with him engendered in her seemed stronger every time. He still filled her and instead of softening after coming so hard inside of her in the shower, she felt his shaft harden once again.

"*Cara*," he murmured. "*Cara* Alexa."

His hips began to move languorously as if he couldn't help himself and the slow slide of him inside of her began to cause the familiar ache, slow steady building of want, need.

She hooked a leg around his waist, sucking from him as he slid in and out of her, his body caressing hers with every stroke. She bowed under him, arms around his neck both legs wrapped around him now. He pulled all the way out and pushed all the way in slowly, steadily as he had in the shower. Out and in, his hips flexed automatically, widening her, filling her with every stroke.

The sensual coupling, the slide of his skin, his body over hers, she drank harder, tears now, springing to her eyes. Safe, filled, pleasured, all her needs met in just this one man. This one person, who was everything she needed, anything she wanted. She felt her body tighten around him again as the climax spiraled around her.

Vaguely, she knew she closed the punctures, murmuring words she couldn't recall.

Chapter Eight

Slowly, carefully, Andrei eased his body away from Alexa, tugging the sheet over her as he backed off the bed. Still bent at the waist, his feet at the floor, he jumped slightly when he felt two hands land on his hips, a denim covered erection pressing against his naked rear. He didn't move but waited, knowing instantly who had invaded his bedroom.

"Your technique is improving, Cousin, but why didn't you finish the job?"

"Adrien," Andrei murmured, standing up straight as his cousin's arms slid around his waist. He turned into the embrace, accepting the hug from the other man and kissing his face. "Shall we take this into the other room? I'd like to leave her sleeping."

"There's no reason why she shouldn't remain sleeping if that's what you want, Andrei," Adrien insisted. "Make her sleep."

Andrei shook his head, threading his fingers through belt loops on either side of his cousin's waist. "I can't do that, Adrien, you know I can't. She needs her free will, especially after tonight."

Adrien cupped Andrei's head in both hands, pulling him in to kiss his forehead, then wrapping one arm around him as he stroked his hair. "Sweet, noble Andrei," he murmured. "Always trying to do things the right way, the fairest way." He guided the dark head to his own shoulder, cousins closer than brothers holding each other in familiarity and comfort.

Andrei allowed himself to be hugged, even cuddled by this, his best friend, his closest cousin. The stinging swat to his bare cheek took him by surprise, snatching his breath away.

"Either clothe yourself, or I'll take mine off, it's all the same to me," Adrien smirked at Andrei who still rubbed the burning handprint he was sure glowed red on his sensitive cheek.

Grumbling under his breath, Andrei stalked into the bathroom, snatched up the black suit pants he favored, and not bothering with underclothes or socks, he jerked them on.

When he returned to the bedroom he found Adrien standing beside the bed, the light sheet lifted in one hand as he surveyed the slumbering Alexa.

Andrei couldn't contain his low growl upon seeing this, causing his cousin to drop the sheet, eyebrow arched. "Not bad, Andrei, not bad," he conceded, causing Andrei's anger to rise another notch.

Not bothering to fasten his pants, Andrei grabbed his cousin by the shoulders and propelled him out of the room. "What do you think you're doing?" he growled, once in the hallway.

"She will soon be one of us," Adrien said, spinning in Andrei's grip to walk backward. "I was merely looking her over."

"She may someday be one of us," Andrei gritted, "but she will be *my* woman, not *our* woman."

"Awww, Andrei," Adrien took his younger cousin's cheek between both palms. "You won't share with me? Your best friend? Your beloved cousin? After all we've been to each other?" his voice held a teasing note.

"Shut up, Adrien," Andrei barked. "No, she is for me, not you."

"Fine." The teasing was gone and Adrien's voice was hard now. "Why have you not changed her then? Why do you leave her subject to that vile bastard's whims?"

"She must be allowed to choose," Andrei growled, incensed. Why was his cousin being so deliberately obtuse?

He stalked over to the en suite bar, fumbling for the wine Naldo always provided him, laced with plasma. Turning he held the bottle up, arching a questioning brow at his cousin.

Naldo nodded, dropping into a chair. "Andrei," his voice was calm now, level. "You can't leave her like this."

Andrei spun from the side bar. "We were forced into what we became," he rasped. "We had no choice but to turn to each other, so many years we were slaves with no rights. I cannot do that to her."

Adrien surged to his feet, moving fluidly across the room to take the wine bottle from the other man. He lay an open palm on the back of Andrei's neck, rubbing lightly, soothing.

"It won't be the same, it isn't the same," his voice was low as he calmed his cousin. "We always had each other and we did learn. But Andrei, when we turned to each other, we three, what happened?" Andrei turned to look at Adrien. "What happened?" his cousin persisted.

At first Andrei thought that Adrien referred to the physical acts of what they'd done. How the three of them had found strength and freedom in each other through the exchange of essence. Looking deeply into the dark eyes, eyes the very image of his own he realized what Adrien was trying to tell him.

"We set one another free. We are linked, but we are free," he breathed.

"Yes," Adrien nodded. "I am here tonight because I chase the old one and I hear his call as you do, as Aiden does. But what compels me is my desire to ruin him, to end him. What compels me still more is your need of me. My need to be here, part of you when you need me."

Andrei leaned his head against Adrien's chest, accepting the comfort and strength from the man he'd known his entire, very long life. They'd been there for each other, he, Adrien, and Aiden. And Adrien was here for him now.

"She wants you for a mate, Andrei, she's frightened, and she needs you. If she wants to walk away at any time…"

"What if I can't let her, Adrien? What if—"

"You are 'Andrei the Honorable'," his cousin chuckled, pinching his cheek. "If she wants to go, you will let her go. Hell, you'll pack her bag and buy her ticket," he concluded snidely.

"Bastard," Andrei's curse sounded more like an affectionate pet name than a vile epitaph.

"Yes, but I'll always be *your* bastard," Adrien chuckled.

Turning from him, Andrei poured them both a glass of the wine, handing one to Adrien.

"How is Aiden?" he asked, moving into the room to settle in a comfortable chair.

"Aiden is as he always was," Adrien responded. "He studies and he broods. He hides away searching, always searching for the way to kill Balfent."

"And you? You do the same. No brooding and studying for you, but trying to kill him yes, that's what you do," Andrei countered.

"Until that diseased vermin is gone, we will never have peace, Andrei," Adrien growled. "You can't doubt that after tonight. So I search him out, I fight him."

"You know that none of us can beat him alone, Adrien. I fear for you, that he'll have you back or worse…"

"Stop, you worry needlessly. I keep him weak. I keep him watching for retribution. It is my constant troubling of him that let you best him tonight."

Andrei sighed. Adrien was probably right, but he worried for him, nonetheless.

"It's late, Adrien. Or early."

"So it is…" Adrien's words were cut off by a gasp at the door. Naldo had returned.

"Many pardons, signore," he apologized. "It is almost like seeing double. I did not expect…" Naldo pulled himself up. "*Scusa.*"

"It's fine, Naldo, please, what have you found?" Andrei stood moving to reassure his servant.

"How can you say we look similar, Naldo?" Adrien leisurely stood as well. "Young Andrei needs to put on some weight. And his hair—a trim perhaps…" he walked up to his younger cousin and ruffled his hair.

Andrei shrugged him off, ignoring him. "Naldo, you have news?" he asked again.

"I located Miss Alexa's servants, *signore.*"

"And? Where Naldo? What was the circumstance?"

Adrien looked on, amused. "She isn't enough for you, Andrei? You need her servants, too?"

"They are important to her. Therefore they are important to me."

"Noble, loving Andrei." Adrien shook his head.

"They were dining—they," Naldo cleared his throat "they dined quite a bit, *signore.* I convinced them that they were tired. They were unable to eat anymore. Perhaps you should look in on them? While it is obvious they are no longer hungry, they seem determined to keep eating."

"I'll go with Naldo, Andrei, and help your friends." Adrien looked pointedly at Andrei. "I will stay with them tonight, to ensure that the old one doesn't return or that he has no more sway over them. You," he angled his head toward the master bedroom. "You see about your mate."

Andrei looked hard at him. Yes, he was right. He would see about her. And the next day, he would talk to her about making their union more permanent.

"Don't just talk to her, Andrei," Adrien said aloud. "Do it."

Chapter Nine

Alexa stirred, the memory of something unpleasant seeping into her consciousness before any real thoughts. She heard herself whimper as if from a long way off and felt two strong arms slide around her.

"Shh, *cara*," Andrei murmured. "All is well, you are safe."

She shifted against him, waking slowly, feeling chilled but not cold really. As the recollections of the night before seeped into her mind, she shuddered, grabbing at him, burrowing into him.

"It was real, wasn't it?" she choked, all of it coming swirling in her brain like a scary movie. Balfent's thrall, his drinking of her blood again and Andrei's nick-of-time arrival, all of it was real, not a dream.

"Yes," Andrei said simply, rocking her in the bed, naked while she was swaddled in the soft sheets.

"You saved me again," she nuzzled against his throat.

"Yes," he said again, looking down at her as she pulled back.

Her gaze captured his and she stared at him for long seconds. "What took you so long, damn it?" She thumped him on the chest with her small fist.

Andrei jerked, more in surprise than pain, certainly. "I had to hunt, Alexa, you know that."

"Hunt," she growled, glaring at him. "You had to go out and stalk prey, trap it and skin it?"

His eyes narrowed on hers. "In fact I *did* have to stalk it and trap it. Skinning it did not prove to be necessary. It isn't as if blood is sold in the grocery store. Or that I can stop by the neighborhood blood bank for a few pints of O positive."

She collapsed against him again. "I'm sorry," she sighed. "I'm being a bitch, I know." She leaned against him for a minute. "I just hate this, I do! My own will subjugated and I'm at the whims of some creep. Like I'm married without being asked. Like—I don't know, it's like my life is tied to his no matter what and I'm just stuck!"

Andrei stirred uncomfortably against her, scooting off the bed. She leaned back, enjoying the view as he stretched, his profile clear in the evening light. She took in the heart pounding sight of his well-muscled profile, bare torso leading down to rippling six pack abs, flat stomach, and curly tufts of satiny black pubic hair. His quiescent penis dangled from it, still respectable size, even at rest. She let her

111

gaze travel down his lightly haired, muscular thighs, well-shaped calves and long, shapely feet. She'd never found feet attractive before. She couldn't control a little smile though as she stared at the hint of hair on the top of his foot and his toes.

Andrei glanced at her and then down at his feet, blushing. "Come, Alexa, we…".

Suddenly it hit her. How could she have forgotten? "Janie! Bernie! Are they? Oh, my god! Andrei!"

She wanted to scream and cry. "What kind of a friend am I?" she moaned. Dropping her head to her hands she went on, "Oh god! I'm no friend, what kind of employer? Oh Andrei!"

Instantly, he was back at the bed, pulling her into his arms, soothing her and comforting her. "Hush, *cara*, hush," he crooned. "They are fine." A firm finger under her chin lifted her face to his. "Do you understand me, Alexa? They are fine. Do you?" he insisted, gripping her chin lightly and giving it a little shake.

She sucked in a deep breath. "Yes, yes, they are fine," she exhaled her relief. "Where were they? What happened to them?"

He smiled faintly, "Naldo found them. The old one was telling you the truth, in his way. They were eating… and eating, and eating. My cousin Adrien is with them now."

"Eating? He made them eat a lot? A *whole* lot?"

"Yes, they were implanted with the idea that they were to keep eating."

"They could have died. They really could have died. And you say they're okay now?" she asked, amazed at the very idea that such a thing was possible. What kind of a creature could make someone eat until they died rather than stop when they were full?

"They are fine, as I said. Naldo found them and my cousin is with them. He will keep watch over them so this cannot happen again," he assured her.

Somehow, she did not feel all that placated. "Your cousin? Your cousin is here? You did mention that you had two cousins who were changed by that evil bastard," she spat. Andrei seemed surprised by her use of the word and his eyes narrowed. She narrowed her eyes in return.

"Yes, I did mention that. Come, let's go see Janie and Bernie and you can meet Adrien."

* * * *

Andrei watched her closely as Alexa preceded him into her penthouse suite. He made eye contact with Adrien but Alexa sailed past him and headed right for Janie who sat on the low couch, looking bemused.

"Janie, Janie, are you okay?" Alexa asked her, concern pouring from her.

"Yes, honey, just…well…bloated. I don't know why I ate so much last night. I never do, you know?" Alexa nodded, concern clear on her face. "Bernie, too. I can't put my finger on it, but somehow I didn't feel right and neither did he. It seemed like eating was the only answer."

"Ohh, Janie," Alexa took the older woman's hand in her own. "How do you feel now? Any better? I know there's a concert tonight but…."

"Oh, honey, I'm fine," Janie tittered, patting Alexa's hand. Her laugh far from reassuring, she was a pale reflection of her usual, ebullient self. "I'm certainly not hungry, but I'll be just fine. Bernie's out walking it off."

Alexa jerked around to look at Andrei, her eyes widening at the sight of Adrien, who arched a mocking brow at her. "Are you sure it's a good idea for Bernie to be out walking right now? Um, I mean— it's…." she couldn't seem to find the right words, and of course Andrei knew what she meant. He understood that the excuse she stuttered out was for Janie's benefit, not his.

"He will be fine," Adrien spoke up. "He's actually only walking (around?) the hotel. And, I know right where he—*probably* is." Alexa stared at him, unblinking. Clearly fighting a smile, Adrien assured her, "I'll just go check on him."

Alexa rose and moved over to the two men. She stared at Adrien for many long seconds. Finally, she extended her hand.

"Alexa, please meet my cousin, Adrien," Andrei introduced them formally.

"My pleasure, Alexa," Adrien took her smaller hand between his two larger ones. "Welcome to the family," he greeted her.

Her face took on a brief moue of confusion and she tugged her hand away. Looking between the two men she observed, "You two sort of—favor each other. Are you related on your mother's side or your father's?"

Adrien graced her with a charming smile as Andrei rolled his eyes. "Our parents were all cousins, but not with each other—it's rather complicated."

"His mother was my father's sister but my mother was Aiden's-- mother's, ah what relation, Adrien?" Andrei had picked up the thread but seemed to trail off. "Yes, it's pretty complicated," he finished lamely.

Alexa laughed and shook her head. "Nice to meet you, Adrien. Thank you for looking after Bernie and Janie for me. They're very important to me."

"My pleasure, Alexa." Adrien smiled politely. To Andrei, he looked like a snake about to spring.

"Andrei, can I speak to you for a second?" Alexa glanced briefly at Adrien and back at Andrei.

"*I don't think she's all that enamored of you, cousin*" Andrei grinned, "Certainly, please, we'll move over here."

He led her toward the foyer. She obviously didn't know that Adrien would likely hear what she had to say anyway. In addition to that, the cousins didn't—couldn't—keep their thoughts from each other. The connection they'd forged to break free of Balfent left them open to each other completely.

When they were away from the others, Alexa turned her worried face to Andrei. "What will happen when I'm on stage tonight? Should we cancel the concert? Will Janie and Bernie be okay? How was he able…?"

Andrei tapped two fingers to her lips lightly, halting the flow of questions. "Calm, Alexa. Shh, it's going to be okay. Balfent was injured and now, Adrien is here to help us. You should be fine."

"*Should* be fine? See…that just doesn't work for me. I want better than that for Bernie and Janie, too. I'm really happy your cousin is here and some other time, I'd really like to ask you about a *million* questions. But right now, the only people who've ever really cared about me are…"

"Hush!" Andrei rapped out. "Listen to me." Alexa crossed her arms over her chest gripping each forearm tightly. She gave him a curt nod. "Balfent did little more than plant an idea in their heads. Adrien will protect them. He won't be able to do it again." Alexa nodded again, acknowledging his statement but not really accepting. "They have cared about you, do care about you. But *cara*, so do I, hmm?"

She released a deep sigh, turning her face away from him. He waited, knowing she was building up to something.

"Andrei, this is so wrong, all of it." She reached for him quickly. "I don't mean you and me—I think, well, I like you. More than like you…It's just that having no choice really bugs me. I just hate not having any place to turn. I don't like that he hijacked me and made me into this—whatever—and now I just have to get used to it. I don't know. I'm all mixed up."

Andrei gently pulled her against him, easing his arms around her. She sighed into his neck, relaxing a little. Slowly, she slipped her arms around his waist.

"I know this has been so awful for you. Can you think of it as being born into a different kind of life?" He struggled to find a way to introduce the exchange of essence to her, but decided that she was just too agitated. He masked his thoughts and concentrated on soothing Alexa's churning fears.

"In time, maybe I can, Andrei," she muttered against his throat, "In time."

"Excuse me," Adrien approached the couple. "I'll go now to see how Bernie is doing, hmm?"

"Thank you." Alexa offered him a weak smile, stepping back from Andrei.

Andrei shook his head as he watched his cousin go.

"Can I have some time with Janie, please?"

Turning back toward the two women, Andrei smiled. "Ladies, I have some phone calls to make. With your permission?"

"Oh, of course Mr. Di Claudio, we'll just sit and chat a bit," Janie answered for both of them.

"Naldo!" Alexa blurted. "Where's Naldo? Is he okay?"

Andrei smiled. For all her ferocity, she really was a caring and softhearted young woman.

"Naldo is fine, Alexa." In four strides, he was leaning over her, pressing a kiss onto her forehead. "He was up rather late last night. I've instructed him to rest for now."

"That's right, honey," Janie chimed in. "He stopped at the restaurant and offered to join us. I still can't imagine why I ate as much as I did. It just seemed so good."

"I'll leave you two for now. Alexa, I will see you before the concert?"

"Yes, of course," Alexa nodded at him, not really even paying him any attention now.

Andrei decided he'd keep his mental ear on the conversation.

* * * *

Alexa lowered herself to the seat beside Janie. Now that they were alone she felt a little uneasy. At first, all she'd wanted was to assure herself that the older couple was fine. Now she wanted to talk to Janie about everything and she just wasn't sure where to start.

Janie apparently knew just what was on her mind, or had some idea, anyway. With a gentle tug to the shoulder, she pulled Alexa against her ample breast and wrapped her in a loving hug.

"We had quite some goings on here last night, didn't we?" Janie asked.

"I don't..." Alexa began.

"I don't either, honey," Janie agreed, "but there was a bit of a mess in your room and out on the balcony. I really can't begin to put my finger on what else took place but I know something has."

Alexa sighed, allowing herself the easy comfort of the other woman's arms.

"You're mostly upset about Mr. Di Claudio though, aren't you?" Not looking at her, Alexa nodded her head against the soft bosom and loving arms. "You're worried about getting too close to him, hmm?" She nodded again. "You've had sex with him?"

Alexa felt her face flame. "Uh, yes, yes, I did."

Janie chuckled. "Maybe you should amend that to *'we had sex with each other',*" she snickered. "Well, I know you think he'll leave you or—or something, don't you?"

"Sort of, Janie, I guess, yeah," she stammered. Was that the biggest part of her problem? Was that what she worried about?

She was a vampire now—or mostly one anyway. If that were the case, well she'd live a good long time. What *was* she really worried her?

"You're worried about falling in love, little girl, aren't you? You're falling in love with that handsome man and you think he's going to just leave you behind, don't you?"

Alexa felt the hot, choking salt of tears clog her throat. Janie was half right. She *was* falling in love with Andrei. But it wasn't his loss that she was feeling now.

"You can't run from love, honey. You have to embrace it," Janie told her, arms tightening. "He seems like a fine man, Alexa, and he really does care about you. Don't cut your nose off to spite your face. Take a chance."

Sniffing loudly, Alexa snuggled even deeper into Janie's warm embrace. "I love you, Janie. Just so you know. I really love you, okay?"

"Oh, sweetheart," Janie sniffed a deep, tearful breath, "I love you, too. And I always knew you loved me, I always did. Look!" she sobbed. "You've got me doing it now!"

Wiping her sleeve across her dripping eyes, Alexa noticed the faint pink of blood tears. She had to get hold of herself. She took a deep breath and thought. In seconds, she was beginning to giggle.

"What the hell does that mean, Janie?" she choked "Why would *anybody* do such a disgusting thing?" She took a deep breath. "Cut your nose off to spite your face...Ewwwww!"

Janie began to giggle right along with her. "I have no idea! My own mother used to say that. Never made a bit of sense to me either!"

Chapter Ten

What would it take?
So far away...
Anything for me?
Anything I'll be Anything

"Very compelling," Adrien murmured, standing next to Andrei in the owner's box, stationed well above the crowd. "She has a lovely voice."

"Yes," Andrei agreed.

"You didn't do it, did you?" Adrien asked. They both knew the question was a formality. While Andrei could block his waking thoughts from Alexa, he could not hide them from Adrien, try though he might.

"Why do you care?" Andrei returned resentfully. "It's not your business how I make love to anyone."

"No," Adrien agreed. "And then again, yes. But she isn't just anyone, is she? She has been branded by Balfent, living the half-life of a vampire—the slave to not one, but two. Your fears and foolish nobility keep her there."

"You overstep yourself, cousin," Andrei growled.

In a flash, Adrien had him by the neck, slamming him against a support column. Pinned by his cousin's hips, Andrei couldn't move. Adrien had always been the stronger.

I don't need Anything,
Not anything you'll see
Anything that keeps you from me
Anything, Anything
You don't need Anything of me

I would do anything
I would give anything
I guess there isn't anything
To keep you with me...

Andrei felt Adrien's hot breath on his face. The other man's lips brushed his as he softly spoke.

"Take her. Change her. If you don't, I will."

Andrei's lips curled back in a feral snarl. "You will not touch her! She is mine!"

Two powerful men, stronger than even the strongest human, pressed tightly together, locked in a hushed battle. "She isn't yours, fool. She's a woman, not a desk lamp," Adrien sneered nipping at Andrei's curled upper lip.

"That is exactly why I won't tie her to me without at least talking to her. She has rights," he hissed in return.

"I thought we settled this." Adrien stepped back, not releasing Andrei but allowing him room. "Her rights include not being a slave to an amoral, animated corpse."

"I simply want to talk to her about it first, that's all." Andrei's head drooped forward and rested against his cousin's chest. He waited. Adrien would know.

"Ohhh, you are a fool, Andrei, aren't you?" his voice was liquid soothing, almost crooning as he petted his cousin's hair. "You never even suggested this to her, did you? She has no idea that the two of you could exchange essence at the same time and she could be free."

"At first, it seemed too much to ask," he mumbled. "Later, I couldn't find the words and she was so angry, so bitter that she'd been changed at all."

Adrien tipped Andrei's head up toward him, a thumb under his chin as he brought their foreheads to rest against each other. "Will it be fifty years of bitter bondage for her, Andrei? I know you want to give her everything, but first give her the freedom to use it. If she hates you for deciding for her, at least she will be free to do so. As it is, she may hate you for leaving her vulnerable to Balfent when you could have spared her. Exchange essence with her, if she's angry, she will have many lifetimes to get over it."

Andrei sighed. "Yes, yes, you're right, Adrien." He opened his mouth to continue when he heard Alexa.

"I don't want to go with him, I don'..."

Both men turned, Andrei alarmed at her thoughts, Adrien no doubt caught by the murmuring of the crowd.

"She just left," they heard. "I've never seen such a thing," another murmur. "Just walked right off the stage..."

* * * *

Andrei went in one direction and Adrien the other, both moving so fast that they were indiscernible to anyone watching. Andrei knew

119

that Balfent could hide his thoughts from them; he was that old and skilled. Alexa couldn't hide anything and that, hopefully, would save her.

"Hush girl," the old one squealed. *"They thought I was down. It takes more than a little bloodletting to keep me from my heart's desire!"*

"Where are we? What is this place? What will you do with me? To me?"

Alexa sounded frightened. Andrei knew that, wherever she was, she wasn't able to speak freely, although her thoughts were still as strong as ever. Did she remember that he'd said that their shared thoughts would be his weakness? He hoped so.

"You, girl, are impudent in the extreme if you actually think I'll answer your silly questions! This place will be your home for now. And I'll do with you as I please," Balfent cackled.

"It's so dirty here," Alexa complained. Was she trying to give a hint as to her whereabouts?

Andrei heard a scream in his head, of alarm certainly, and possibly pain. Had the old devil hit her?

"You have enough of her blood to find her, don't you?" Adrien had met him in the parking garage. The hope that the old monster had kept her nearby sizzled away before they'd given it credence.

"Yes, of course I do," Andrei snapped, angrier with himself than Adrien. He squeezed his cousin's hand briefly as both men slid in under the rising doors one either side of the yellow Lamborghini.

The enormous 530 BHP engine rumbled to life as Andrei shifted it into gear, carefully, and backing out of the secluded parking slot. He glanced at Adrien, exchanging an embarrassed grin that they both could so love this supercar, even at so urgent a time.

Instinctively, he turned the yellow beast into traffic and let himself trust that he'd find her.

Chapter Eleven

Alexa was frightened, without a doubt but she couldn't fight the moment of inner irritation that she was so soon in this position again. Truthfully, she hadn't been in this *exact* position before, but she was at the mercy of that nasty vampire again, and that just made her mad.

She'd read so many books, seen so many movies, but the reality was surreal on so many levels. Here she was, in what seemed to be a dilapidated warehouse, musty and certainly, rat infested. She really couldn't control her own body, she was a prisoner inside her mind, but she did have awareness. Right now, she counted that among her blessings, but for how long?

The old predator didn't seem to want her sexually. At least he didn't seem to want that right *now*, she revised. Would he later? She knew he could hear her thoughts and she tried to direct them away from Andrei. Well, she wanted to let Andrei know where she was and what was going on, but how to do that without tipping their hand?

"Ewww, rats!" she complained. *"Is that what you had for dinner last night? Besides me, I mean—there must not be a lot of people way out here."*

"Silence, woman! You are mine and you will *not* invade my thoughts..."

The old guy actually seemed pretty frazzled. She wondered for a moment if vampires could get senile dementia. If it was possible to feel a smile in your head, Alexa was certain Andrei had smiled at her dry sense of humor. She had always looked at things in her own unorthodox way, her thoughts skipping from idea to solution to new events like a bee searching flowers.

Right now, though, resting on her butt, propped on her scraped palms at the back of a dank and dusty warehouse, unorthodox thoughts were all that was keeping her sane.

"I have her now, boy!" Balfent screamed, his voice echoing through the empty cavern of crumbling wood and tin. "You think you hurt me *but I have her!*" he bellowed, the screech resonating around the building and disturbing a small colony of bats hanging in the rafters.

Yep, she thought, *looks like the creepy old bastard finally let go of that last working brain cell...*

"I am *not* crazy you insolent wench!" he rounded on her, drawing his arm back to strike her again.

The rumble of the Lamborghini's purring engine stayed his hand, causing him to whirl away and then back again. Without a word, he snatched her against him, moving faster than anything she could imagine. Though he seemed a frail older man, teetering on the brink of sanity, his physical strength was enormous. He lifted her as if she weighed no more than one of the rats she'd accused him of snacking on.

Before she could think, they emerged from the building, plunging into the dark and chilly night.

Giving up all pretense of protection, she cried out mentally, *"ANDREI! Help me!"*

* * * *

Andrei shifted the big car into neutral, turning at a slow angle the moment he spotted the deserted warehouse.

"I'll get him, you get her," Adrien murmured, unsnapping his seatbelt manually.

"You'll need help, cousin," Andrei protested, though not as ardently as he would in the past.

"I think *you'll* need help." Adrien grinned at him, his white teeth flashing in the light of the dashboard.

"Funny, very funny," Andrei shot him a smile as they simultaneously released the rising doors on either side. "I hope this doesn't mess up my paint job," Andrei groaned.

"At least your priorities are ordered properly," Adrien laughed as he jumped.

Andrei jumped to the other side, both men rolling to their feet and turning in the same direction. He heard Alexa's mental scream for help and tried to reassure her without tipping Balfent to the knowledge that they were so near.

Doubtless, his concerns were wasted he was sure. Balfent was their maker; he would know they were near.

"Tree, Andrei, a giant, twisted..." her thoughts just cut off and Andrei felt terror twist his insides. Could Balfent still kill her? She was more vampire than not but...she wasn't completely changed. Why, oh why, hadn't he coupled with her and shared essence to guarantee her a future and a choice. Why?

"Stop it, Andrei, stop," Adrien cut his thoughts short as they neared the tree she'd begun to describe.

Andrei could see her crumpled body at the base of the tree, a vivid mark on her forehead attesting to the fact that she'd impacted the trunk of the tree, or some other hard and stationary object, with great force.

"Look at my two beautiful boys," Balfent sneered. "Come to see me? You miss me? And look what I have to play with…." he taunted.

Andrei stepped closer as Adrien moved several paces to the left. "Why must you terrorize innocent women?" Andrei asked sadly.

It couldn't be that much of a mystery that he was keeping the old vampire busy. Still, he was hurt, run down, perhaps temporarily insane, if such a thing were possible.

"Why wouldn't I, boy? I have her and here you are. She's perfect because she drew you to me." Balfent stepped away from Alexa's still form. He stared hard at Andrei, no doubt trying to mesmerize him. "You were always my favorite, Andrei. So sweet, so soft hearted. So loving. Even a jaded old soul such as I need that from time to time."

The high voice had changed from a sneer to a wheedle as he moved just a little closer to Andrei. Out of his periphery, Andrei saw Adrien move up and out. *He* tried not to think of what his cousin was doing. He kept his mind fixed firmly on Alexa and nothing else.

She wasn't moving, perhaps not even breathing—would that matter? Could she be resuscitated?

"You can have her if you like, Andrei," the voice was soft as a feather stroking his senses. Musically, it drifted over him and he stepped forward. "She can be yours—there for you whenever you want her. Isn't she lovely? Don't you want to keep her safe?"

Wrestling against the urge to move closer, Andrei lifted his head, closed his eyes, and imagined his cousins, both Aiden and Adrien. He pictured the steps they'd taken to save each other, to save all three. He imagined making love with Alexa, safe in a secluded home, well away from the evil old creature taunting him now.

The sound of a wet, crunching impact wrenched his eyes open just before Balfent's scream of rage and pain split the air. "Go, Andrei!" Adrien shouted, his muscular arms wrapped around the vile old fiend. "Run! Get her and run!"

As if released from a trance, Andrei sprang forward, some part of him torn, wanting to sprint after his cousin.

"No, Andrei, he is injured. I am fine. See to her, see!"

"Adrien, you'll need me! None of us can best him alone!"

"I won't best him, Andrei, I'll keep him running, keep him weak. Get her and get away. Trust me, I won't allow him to hurt me. Trust me."

Adrien was running still, long gone, Andrei knew. *"Promise me,"* he insisted, knowing that it was a moot point now, but needing the words anyway.

"Noble Andrei," his cousin was enjoying this, the chase, the hunt, Andrei realized. Adrien loved risk, thrived on it. *"Take care of the woman, let me have my fun."*

"Tell me when you've settled somewhere, hmm?" Andrei was at the base of the tree now. Stretching his arm out to her, he was sure he'd know instinctively if Alexa lived or not. What if she was dead—she was too new, she could still die.

His heart slammed painfully against his chest, he could taste rusty fear on the back of his tongue. Shaking, he touched her, hooking two fingers in the torn fabric of her bodice and pulling her to roll toward him. He reached to brush the hair away from her bruised face, blood oozing from the broken skin. The skin under his fingers was clammy, cool to his touch. He felt a jolt of dread beat against his ribs, shocking, painful.

She was bleeding. Dead people didn't bleed, right? Stroking her throat with the tips of his fingers, he found her sluggish pulse. She was injured and badly. Could she live?

"Alexa?"

"Mmm?"

She heard him! She was aware. Somewhat aware, he amended to himself. He lifted her, moving with all speed, away from the cold, hard ground, away from the twisted tree. But where? Where could he take her? There, bright gold reflecting the white glow of the full moon, his car. He laid her carefully on the wide hood that stretched to cover the powerful engine. Seconds had passed from the time he lifted her and when he stretched beside her on the glossy yellow hood.

"Alexa," he murmured to her. "I must finish the change. If I don't you'll die." He couldn't' tell if he was thinking or speaking or both. "Alexa, I can't let you die."

She didn't answer and he worried that he'd waited too long. Her face seemed soft still, the skin cool but not cold, supple.

"Don't leave me, Alexa, I want you with me," he murmured. "All this time, and I found someone to love, don't die."

Gathering her still form against his body, Andrei turned his head and bit into his bicep, tearing the large vein that traveled to his shoulder. With no finesse, he angled her so that her lips pressed against the gushing wound.

After a very few seconds, he felt her mouth open of its own accord, her lips and tongue moving on the torn flesh. Now he felt her dainty fangs puncture his skin, pinpricks and then the sensual feeling of her mouth working on him, suckling at his vein, drinking his blood.

When he began to feel the heat build in her, the temperature of her skin rise, he carefully lay her down on the rocky and uneven ground. His tongue traced the side of her elegant throat, opposite the arm from which she drank. He lathed the silken surface, reveling in the warm, spicy, sweet taste of her. His tongue stroked up, down, and he buried his sharp incisors in the now pulsing hot vein.

"Will you stay with me, Alexa? Is it possible that you love me?" He had to ask while he could still think. Somewhere between the joy of her living still and the erotic sensations of her lips, her teeth, teasing and milking him as he did the same, he could barely think.

"Yes, Andrei, I will stay with you. And it is completely possible that I love you. I'm not good at it, though." Was she sure, he thought? Could she be in some kind of thrall?

"Cut it out! I'd be under his *thrall if I was—you know I don't like that word. What do I have to do to stay with you? To love you for all time? What—what does it take?"*

"We make love while we drink from each other. We will go and..."

"No!" she insisted. *"Now! We're already drinking. I don't want to go another step without us both knowing what we are to each other. Please, Andrei. I want you now."*

Her hands were fumbling at his zipper as she spoke to him, thought to him, she slid her tongue on the sweaty, salty skin of his bicep, teasing him as one leg hooked around his own. This action caused the full skirt of her lightweight dress to slide up her bare leg, leaving her almost completely open to him. She wriggled against his hip, sliding a little on the warming hood of the car. Her fingers were busy, attempting to slide the satin of her thong aside, in order to be completely ready for him. He could already smell the excitement building in her. In spite of the traumatic events she'd experienced this night she wanted him.

Both had slowed in their supping though they still suckled from each other, drinking the hot essence as they did. Andrei's large hand covered Alexa's smaller feminine fingers, guiding his zipper down. He reached to lift her skirt still more as she slipped her fist into his pants and pulled his now full shaft out.

"Feel me, Andrei. How hot you make me every time I touch you this way. How did I live so long without you and without this?"

"Silly little thing." His finger slipped under the strip of satin, stroking the moist labia waiting there. *"You have barely lived at all."*

His finger slid into her, finding her wet and clinging, her heavy cream testifying to her readiness for him.

"Please, Andrei, don't torment me," he heard her whimper.

She arched into him as her fingers slipped under his engorged cock, stroking and teasing at his felt soft sacks. Now Andrei had to fight a groan, holding her open and guiding his throbbing length into her. He felt her bottom teeth scraping the skin below the bite as both legs wrapped tightly around his waist. One hand cupped her head, protecting her from the thick windshield glass as they shifted. The other rested under her as she drank.

He had a lifetime to pinch and fondle her nipples, to enjoy the moonlight on her skin. For now, he pulled his hips back, loving the smooth, tight slide of his length deep inside of her wet channel. In. Out. So hot, so tight, so wet, their bodies sliding on the warm, wide hood of the Lamborghini, cool air caressing their hot, yielding flesh. He felt her clamping around him, his cock seeming to grow wider, longer, thicker inside of her, her tongue teasing him and her legs a beautiful vice around his hips.

His balls felt tight, the tingling starting deep inside and sparking up his spine as he pumped steadily at first but now more and more erratically in and out of her. Her legs squeezing ever tighter and the hot essence, the nectar of her blood flowing into his mouth as his flowed into her he couldn't hold back. He couldn't slow down. Harder and harder he thrust and she thrust back, pulling away and meeting him, hot bodies skating over the slick, glossy paint, the hard, wet smack of their bodies echoing down the hill and around the deserted valley. Then the gushing, pounding wave took him, took them both. He could feel her channel squeezing, convulsing around him, milking every drop of cream from him until he knew he was empty. He couldn't think, could barely breathe.

Carefully, he lifted his mouth from her throat, licking the small nicks closed. Following his lead, Alexa did the same, closing the tear and the small incisions made by her little fangs. He gathered her against him, holding her close, reluctant to move.

"Andrei?" her voice was low and serious, almost somber.

"Yes, *cara*?" He wasn't sure he wanted to hear what was coming.

"Why didn't you tell me? About the essence thing?" He couldn't look away from her dark and accusing eyes. "It could have saved us both, even spared Bernie and Janie."

"I was afraid that you were under my influence and couldn't judge fairly." He took a deep breath. "Perhaps it was foolish of me. I confess that, in my own way, I was afraid."

"Afraid?" She tilted her head, questioning. "Afraid of what?"

"I was afraid that you wouldn't want me if you had a choice." Andrei felt the heat creep up his face. "I thought you'd perhaps blame me for this terrible thing that had befallen you, or that maybe you'd think it wasn't real, that you were in my thrall. It was fear, I know. And because I didn't want to face the possibility that you wouldn't forgive me, I almost lost you."

She rubbed her cheek against his. "Sometimes I just can't believe men," she murmured. "That was stupid, you know that?"

"*Told you, cousin!*" Adrien's echoing laughter resounded in his thoughts.

He grinned, embarrassed. "Yes, I know."

"*I have got to get me a car like that,*" Adrien added from wherever he was. Andrei firmly put him out of his mind.

A slight shift, maybe by both, dislodged his shrinking member from her heat and with it, a gush of his seed spilled out to stain the bright yellow finish of their unlikely love nest.

"The wet spot," she smirked.

"The wet spot?" he murmured, feeling a smile in every part of him. "What exactly do you mean?"

"I saw it on a TV show," she said and grinned. "The guy was complaining that his wife always made him sleep in the wet spot." She considered him carefully for a moment. "Hey, are you going to marry me? Or are we going to live in sin for all eternity?"

He pretended to think it over. "Well, you do seem to be conspicuously short of a last name." He rolled until she was on top of him, adjusting her skirt as he did. "Suppose we do both?"

"Live in sin *and* get married? Can we do that?" Her breathless voice made it sound as if he'd suggested they fly to the moon on a balsa wood airplane.

"We can do whatever you want to do, *Cara mia*," Andrei murmured, sitting up now, cradling her in his lap as he tucked his genitals back into his pants. "We have all of eternity to make up whatever rules we choose."

He was surprised to see sadness cross her face as her head dipped away from him. "Alexa?" he asked, very confused.

"I love you, Andrei. I'm sure I'm going to love you forever. I just…I'm sure because I can't imagine not loving you now."

"But?" he asked, tipping her face up with one finger.

"But I love Bernie and Janie and…." She sniffed lightly and he could tell she was fighting tears. "How do you live with seeing people you love grow old and die? How?"

"Shh," he soothed her. "You live with them, you love with them, you spend each minute with them doing anything you can to show them how precious they are every moment you have. You rail against the ill fate that would take them and you remember that the natural order of things is to live and die, as someday we must. And you love those who love you and take comfort in them, always."

"And now, we can do it together." She pushed herself up, hands on his shoulders and twitching her skirt as she did.

In one smooth motion, he slid from atop the car to stand, lifting her against him as he did. "Now we can do *anything* together."

I would do anything
I would give anything
I guess there isn't anything
To keep you with me…

Epilogue

Adrien d'Coludi glanced around the crowded room, ignoring the tittering women and intense, focused men. These innocent fools thought that every social climb, every business meeting, these were their goals, their driving force. Little did they know that death walked among them.

He himself would leave one, more than one of them weak and confused before the night was over. And this night, he was feeling hungry, mean. He had that empty, clawing feeling, that itch.

Someone would feel both his tooth and his cock tonight. Man or woman? He'd know when the right one stumbled across his path. By and large he preferred a sweet smelling, soft woman, and the selection was plentiful tonight.

Yes, a woman. What flavor? Redhead? Brunette? Blonde? Hmmm, he felt like a redhead tonight. Before he allowed his eyes to land on his lucky choice, he heard it--the familiar leaking hiss of Balfent's thoughts.

"You think you'll find a dining companion, boy? Someone to share your bed for the night? Poor Adrien, locked forever in a cat and mouse game with me. And you call Sweet Andrei noble. Look at you! What fun can there be? Chasing an old man like me and never hoping to win? What will you give to beat me? It will cost you everything boy, everything you have." The demented cackle resounded in his head; he shook it imperceptibly.

Adrien sneered, glancing around, knowing the old one wasn't far, possibly even watching him. *"You took everything from me years ago, old fiend. And now, everything is a small price to pay to keep you ill and worried. A very small price, indeed."*

Yes, a redhead, he decided, one of his weaknesses. With a curl of his lips, he slid in behind an expensively, if scantily, clad young woman. Pulling her against his burgeoning erection, his hand slid up her bare thigh.

"You want that, darling?" he murmured in her ear.

"Uhh," she gasped.

His fingers slid between her legs and under the scrap of materiel covering her weeping sex.

"Your body says you do. What about the rest of you?" He stroked her lower lips with one finger.

"Yes," she sighed. "Um, yes."

Adrien smiled and licked the pulse at her throat. *Yes.* He couldn't fight the old bastard every second, now could he?

The End